LASSOED BY FORTUNE

MARIE FERRARELLA

To

Susan Litman,

who somehow manages

the monumental task of

keeping all these stories

straight

while keeping us all

in line.

Chapter One

Liam Jones leaned back in his chair, nursing his beer and listening to two of his younger brothers, Jude and Toby, talking about a third younger brother, Christopher, who had recently picked up and moved to the nearby town of Red Rock.

As he listened, Liam's frown, already a fixture on his face from the beginning of this conversation, deepened, highlighting his increasing disapproval.

Christopher, apparently, at least in his eyes, had gone and sold his soul to the devil.

Liam's initial intent in coming to the bar at the Horseback Hollow Grill with two of his brothers was to unwind a little. Instead as he listened to Toby and Jude, he found himself getting progressively more and more annoyed. The current discussion was merely a theme and variation of the same old thing; a topic that had taken center stage in his family for months now: his mother's rediscovered wealthy siblings.

Liam had always known his mother, Jeanne Marie, had been adopted and, like her, he'd thought nothing of it. Countless people were adopted; it was no big thing. Just this past year his own brother Toby had taken in three foster children.

What made it such a big thing, not just in his eyes but in everyone else's, was that it turned out his mother had been given up for adoption, along with a sister she hadn't even known about until just recently, by none other than a member of the highly revered Fortune family.

And that little bit of news had turned all of their worlds upside down.

The ironic thing was that his mother might have very well gone to her grave not knowing a thing about her roots if her brother, James Marshall Fortune, hadn't come poking around, telling her that she was not only his sister but that she, he and the sister she had previously known nothing about—a British woman named Josephine May—were actually triplets.

The whole thing sounded like something out of a movie and if it had been a movie, he would have walked out on it right in the middle. Specifically around the part where this "long-lost brother" of hers gave her a whole wad of money. That had been James Marshall's way of "making it up to her" for having lived a life that hadn't been embedded in the lap of luxury.

As if money could fix everything and anything.

Liam found the whole money thing offensive and degrading. He resented the offering of a "consolation prize" to make up for the fact that his mother had lived a life that James Fortune obviously felt was beneath her.

When his mother gave Fortune back his money, Liam had never been prouder of her. But then she'd gone and spoiled it all by turning around and asking him and his siblings to not just recognize these interlopers as their blood relatives but to actually take on their surname.

Oh, they'd still be the Jones family, but now they'd all be known as the *Fortune* Joneses.

The hell they would, Liam thought angrily as he took another swig of his beer, which by now was decidedly no longer cold. But he hardly noticed.

In all honesty, he had expected his six siblings to feel *exactly* the way he did and was utterly stunned to discover that the whole thing didn't even *begin* to bother them as much as it did him.

In fact, it felt as if his brothers and sisters were dropping like flies around him, taking on the Fortune name and forgetting just who the hell they were to begin with: Deke Jones's offspring.

Granted, their father wasn't an emotional, verbally effusive man. But at the same time, he was a decent, hardworking man who had always made sure they had food in their bellies, a roof over their heads and more opportunity to make something of themselves than he had. Some men showed they cared by talking, others by doing. Deke Jones fell into the latter category.

Liam sensed that this rush to embrace the Fortune

name was a slap in the face for his father, even though
Deke had said nothing about it either way.

But the look in his eyes certainly did.

As the conversation continued to revolve around
Christopher and his drastic move out of town, Liam
found that his temper had been brought dangerously
close to the edge and was about to flare.

"You know, it's like he's not even the same person
anymore," Toby observed about the absent member of
their family. "When this whole thing started, Christopher hated the Fortunes as much as we did. Now he's
run off to Red Rock to work for them. I just don't get
it," Toby, who at twenty-eight was the youngest of the
three of them, confessed, shaking his head.

Jude shrugged carelessly. "Oh, they're not so bad,"
he told Toby, defending this newly uncovered branch
of the family. Blessed with a keen survival instinct, he
deliberately avoided looking in Liam's direction. Jude
knew what his thirty-two-year-old brother thought of
all the Fortunes and the last thing he was looking for
was a fight. He just wanted to impart the information
he'd learned about these new relatives of theirs. After
all, fair was fair.

"Gabriella knows them," Jude went on, referring to
his fiancée, "and she said that they're good people who
just got a raw deal, bad-mouthed by folks who're just
jealous of their success and their money." He spared one
quick, fleeting glance in Liam's direction to see how he
was taking this and then just as quickly looked away.
"You know how some people are. They try to drag down

anyone who's doing better than they are, thinking that might somehow elevate them."

Liam had heard enough. Fed up, he slammed his beer mug down on the table with such force, the sound reverberated loudly enough to garner him a few curious looks from people seated at the nearby surrounding tables, not to mention the attention of several other patrons.

"Oh, come *on*." Liam ground the words out angrily. "Wake up and smell the coffee, guys. Anyone saying anything good about those people is just trying to cozy up to their fat bank accounts and their fancy circle of friends. The Fortunes *use* people. Anyone who thinks different is just fooling themselves."

Toby felt that his brother was forgetting a very important point in all this. "But Mom says—" he began.

Liam waved his hand at his younger brother before the latter could say anything further.

"I love Mom, but she's just being emotional right now and I don't fault her for that. But I'm a 'Jones' boy. Not 'Fortune Jones,' just plain old 'Jones' and I'm proud of it, proud of the old man, of having a father who worked hard to make a life for himself and his family. And I'm not about to change the way I feel just because some rich guy comes along and tells us we're the missing branch of his family. Who knows if he's even telling her the truth, anyway?"

"Why would he lie about something like that?" Toby wanted to know.

"Hell if I know," Liam answered with a shrug. "Who knows why people like that do anything? Maybe there's something in it for them that we don't know about yet."

Which, to him, was all the more reason why they should view the whole scenario suspiciously. That way, they wouldn't be wide open if something *did* happen.

Jude gave him a steely look. "You're reaching, Liam. It doesn't matter what you feel or don't feel. That doesn't change any of the facts—and the facts are you've got Fortune blood running through your veins. We all do. Face it, big brother, you're a Fortune."

Liam held up his hand, as if to physically stop the flow of words that could only lead to a knock-down, drag-out argument between them. Clearly nothing was going to be resolved here by talking about those people.

Deep down in his soul, he really felt that if by some wild chance he and his family welcomed these people with open arms, the Fortunes would only wind up infecting them with their greed.

With that in mind, it was best just to change the subject and talk about something else.

"How much longer are you planning on hanging on to those Hemings kids?" he asked Toby. "I mean, don't you think that five months is plenty?"

"Not really," Toby answered. "I haven't exactly figured out what I'm doing yet. But just so you know," he told Liam, "I *like* having those kids around. They make me see things differently."

Liam laughed shortly. That certainly wouldn't have been the way he would have felt about having three children infiltrating every corner of his life.

"To each his own, I guess," he told Toby. "As for

me, I don't like being responsible for anyone else but myself."

"Yeah, we already know that," Toby commented dryly. "That's not exactly a news flash."

"If I were you, I wouldn't go boasting about that too much," Jude warned Liam. "The gods have a way of taking you down a peg or two if they think you're being too happy—or too irreverent," Jude pointed out. And then, as if not to leave Toby out, he couldn't help commenting, "You know that being responsible for three kids can't be doing much for your social life."

"Why don't you let me worry about my social life," Toby told Jude in a laid-back tone.

Jude turned toward Liam. "Speaking of social life, how's yours been lately? You seem a little…I don't know, solitary these days," he said. "I can remember a time when you had to beat girls off with a stick."

"I do just fine, thanks, Jude." He grinned. "I've learned not to beat them off anymore."

Liam had always been devoted to working on his ranch from sunup to sundown—and then some.

"Just remember—both of you," Jude said, looking from one brother to the other. "Don't underestimate the value of having a good woman at your side."

Liam drained his mug, setting it down again. He had to be getting back soon. As always, there was work to be done.

But he wasn't ready to leave just yet. "God, Jude, ever since you got engaged to that little Mendoza girl, you're acting whipped."

"Don't let Gabriella hear you call her a little girl," Jude warned seriously. "She's certainly more woman than you ever went out with—except for maybe that Julia Tierney."

Something within Liam tensed at the mere mention of Julia's name. It always did. Everyone had at least one person they thought of as "the one that got away." Julia was his.

"He never went out with Julia," Toby told Jude.

Jude looked a little confused. "I thought Liam asked every girl in his senior class out," Jude said.

"He did ask," Toby answered, keeping a straight face. "But Julia was the only one with the good sense to turn him down." He turned his sharp blue eyes on Liam. "That wounded your fragile pride, didn't it, big brother?"

"Shut up, both of you," Liam ordered in a flat, emotionless voice. "And for the record, my pride's not fragile and it wasn't wounded. Not going out with me was Julia's loss, not the other way around," he informed his brothers in a no-nonsense voice.

He saw Toby's mouth drop open and wondered why since he hadn't exactly said anything earth-shattering or that novel for that matter. The next moment, both his brothers were scrambling to their feet, as if, belatedly, to show their respect.

"Funny, I remember it the other way around," a melodic female voice behind Liam's chair said.

Caught off guard, Liam swung around so fast he almost caused his chair to tilt and deposit him on the sawdust floor. He managed to steady the chair at the very last moment, preventing a spill and a great deal of embarrassment on his part.

The object of their conversation was smiling a greeting at his brothers.

Julia had stopped by the Horseback Hollow Grill with a definite agenda in mind. The Grill was the town's only restaurant and she had just happened upon a situation that could very well enable her to bring a second eatery to the small town.

She had been looking at The Grill with fresh eyes, as if she'd never seen the place before, when she'd heard Liam Jones making a commotion as he banged down his mug. Curiosity had prompted her to move closer to his table to find out what was going on. Ordinarily she would have kept to herself, but she was feeling hopeful about her future for the first time in a long time, so she'd decided to indulge herself and find out what the man was carrying on about.

He had certainly changed a lot since their high school days, she couldn't help thinking. His build had gotten way more muscular and his tan appeared to be permanent, no doubt from his days on the ranch. But what he had gained in looks, he had lost in temperament. From the little bit she had caught, he sounded as though he was well on his way to becoming a grumpy old man, not the exciting, wild-eyed bad boy she had known in high school.

"Hello, boys. How are you?" she asked, looking at Toby and Jude. Then, as they nodded, offering almost a synchronized chorus of "Fine, how are you?" she looked at Toby. Her blue eyes crinkled as she asked, "How are the kids, Toby?"

"They're doing great, thanks for asking," Toby told her, beaming.

She didn't leave it there, although she knew she could have. But she was serious in asking after the children Toby had selflessly taken in—surprising a lot of people—and she wanted Toby to be aware of something.

"You're doing a good thing, Toby, taking those children in like that," she said warmly. "Kids need to feel wanted. It anchors them."

So now she was dispensing child-rearing advice? Liam thought. Well that went with the territory, didn't it? Julia had always acted as if she felt she was above him and, by association, above his family, as well.

"Since when did you start dabbling in child psychology?" Liam asked, acutely aware that the one girl in high school who had actually hurt his budding male ego was still going out of her way to ignore him. And even more acutely aware that no matter how much he tried not to let it bother him—it did.

"That's not psychology, that's just common sense, Jones—or should I say Fortune Jones?" she asked, the corners of her mouth curving as she looked at him.

"Might just be wiser not to say anything at all," Liam countered.

Jude and Toby exchanged looks and pushed their chairs in against the table.

"I think that's our cue to leave," Jude said to his younger brother. He then tipped the rim of his hat to Julia. "Nice seeing you again, Julia."

"Yeah, see you around," Toby echoed his brother, tipping his own hat belatedly.

Liam waited until his brothers had walked out of the bar before he said, "If you're expecting to hear the same from me, you're going to have to wait until hell freezes over."

Rather than be affronted, Julia smiled up at Liam. "I've never expected anything from you, Liam, except exactly what you delivered. Which was nothing," she added after a beat in case there was any question as to her meaning.

He was *not* about to take the bait, he told himself. Instead he said mildly, "Been sharpening that tongue of yours, I see."

Julia inclined her head. "I guess you just bring out the worst in me, Jones."

He appeared unfazed by her assessment. "I didn't know there was anything else to bring out," he replied mildly.

"Is that why you asked me out that time in high school?" she questioned with a knowing smile. She had been more than a little attracted to him at the time, but he had always had all these simpering girls around him, ready to do anything he asked just to be with him. It had been enough to turn her completely off. There was absolutely no way she would have *ever* allowed herself to be part of an adoring crowd, a devoted groupie like the others. Liam had had a large enough ego back then without her adding to it.

"Anyone else would have realized that I'd asked you out because I didn't want you to feel left out and wonder if there was something wrong with you. I didn't want to hurt your feelings."

"There's a difference between being left out of a crowd and being superior to the crowd. You seemed to thrive on having all those girls fawn over you and, frankly, I never saw what all the attraction was so I never wanted to join that very limited club," she informed him. There was no way in heaven she'd admit to being attracted to him then—and she was even more unwilling to admit that the attraction had never really faded away.

His eyes narrowed, pinning her down. "For someone who didn't want to join the club, I sure caught you looking at me enough times," he recalled.

"Yes, I looked at you," she admitted. "But if you'd actually looked back at me, you would have realized that was pity in my eyes, not admiration." She shook her head, her long, straight hair moving like a mesmerizing red cloud as it framed her face. "But you just assumed that all the girls were so crazy about you."

This could go on for hours. Though he would have never admitted it out loud, they were pretty evenly matched and he wasn't about to get the best of her any time soon. She might not have anything else to do— since she was obviously not rushing back to the grocery store she managed for her ailing father—but he had a ranch to run.

"I don't have time for this," he declared abruptly.

"You never did have time for the truth," he heard her say as he turned his back on her and walked out of the bar.

It took Liam a while to cool down. Longer than the trip back to the ranch. Julia Tierney was the one person in town who could raise his blood pressure to dangerous heights with no effort at all.

She could also do the same thing to his body temperature.

Chapter Two

As was her custom six days a week, Julia came down from the small apartment above the store where she lived at exactly 7:00 a.m. to unlock the front door to the Horseback Hollow Superette, the town's only grocery store, which had been in her family for several generations. It was also the only grocery store for thirty miles.

The store served its customers from seven until seven Monday through Saturday. On Sundays, the hours were somewhat shorter. However, since Julia did live just above the grocery store, she could *always* be reached in case someone had a "food emergency" of some sort—such as relatives showing up for a forgotten dinner just when the cupboard was bare.

Running the family business had *not* been what she'd envisioned doing with her life when she had been a senior in high school, but this was—at least for now—the plan that *life* seemed to have in store for her.

Twelve years ago she had been all set to go away to an out-of-state college with an eye out to someday perhaps owning her own restaurant. She'd loved to cook ever since she could reach the top of the stove without the benefit of using a stool. She could still remember the very first thing she had prepared for her parents: cinnamon toast. At four she'd been proud enough to burst at what she'd viewed to be a major accomplishment: toast buttered on both sides with a dusting of cinnamon.

Her parents had been nothing but encouraging and supportive from the start, telling her there wasn't anything she couldn't do or become if she set her mind to it.

And then, just like that, her world had come crashing down all around her.

Right before she was to leave for her first semester at college, her father had had a heart attack. For a while it was touch and go and the doctors weren't sure if he would pull through. There was no way she could leave him or her mother at a time like that.

And even when her father began to come around, she found more than a ton of reasons that kept her right where she was. Between concern over her father's health and trying to keep up her mother's morale—not to mention because her parents needed the income to pay for her father's medical bills—there was no way she could find the time to go away to school. Her family needed her too much and she'd refused to leave them high and dry.

Though they always had part-time help at the Superette, there was really no one else to keep things going. Math had always been her mother's undoing.

So Julia had stayed on, putting her dream on hold— which sounded a good deal better to her than saying that she was giving up her dream—and doing what needed to be done.

Looking back now, that almost seemed like a lifetime ago to her.

With time, her father, Jack, had improved somewhat, although he was never again the hale-and-hearty man he'd been before the heart attack. And eventually, she'd seen the color come back into her mother's face to the point that Annie Tierney no longer looked as if she was auditioning for the part of a ghost.

As for herself, she'd gone from being a carefree, whimsical young girl to being a practical, pragmatic young woman with the weight of the world occasionally on her shoulders.

But she managed. She *always* managed.

Those years had also seen her married and then divorced, neither of which happened with a great deal of emotion or fanfare. Marrying Neal Baxter, a local boy who had just returned to Horseback Hollow to practice law after getting his degree, seemed like the right thing to do at the time. She and Neal were friends and Julia had honestly believed that having a friend to go through life with was a smart thing to do.

But a few years into the marriage, a marriage that seemed to be built on little more than mutual respect and a whole lot of boredom, she and Neal came to the conclusion that they really liked one another far too much to be trapped in something that promised no joy to either of them.

So an uncontested, amicable divorce settlement was quickly and quietly reached. They each came away with whatever they had brought into the marriage.

It was a case of no harm, no foul, except that Julia had learned that dreaming about things you couldn't have—such as a passionate marriage—really *did* hurt.

After that, the store became her haven, her home base. It was the one thing she could always depend on to be there. After a time her job became so ingrained she went about her day's work routine practically on autopilot.

Before unlocking the door, she first prepared the store for customers. Produce was put out and carefully arranged in the appropriate bins. The breads, pastries and especially the doughnuts were baked fresh every morning—she saw to that even though it meant she had to get up extremely early to get the goodies to the store in time to arrange the display. It was her one creative outlet and she looked forward to the scents of sugar and butter in her kitchen each morning.

Aside from that, there were always a hundred different little details to see to and Julia kept a running checklist in her head at all times, making sure she hadn't forgotten anything.

She did all this by herself and even, at times, found the solitude of the store comforting at that hour.

So when she saw her mother in the store, Julia was more than a little surprised. Her mother was sweeping the aisles, a chore Julia normally took care of just before opening, a full hour before she normally came in. Annie always arrived *after* having made breakfast for her husband.

Judging by her presence—not to mention the look on her mother's face—something was definitely up.

Julia approached the problem—because there *had* to be a problem—slowly by asking, "Mom, what are you doing here?"

Looking far from her normally sunny self, Annie answered, "It's my store. I work here. Or have you forgotten?"

"I *know* you work here, Mom," Julia said patiently, "but you don't come in until after eight. Everything okay with Dad?" she asked, suddenly concerned.

Julia realized that was the only thing that would make her mother break with her regular routine. Her mother was nothing if not a creature of habit. It was Annie who had taught her that a regular routine would give her life structure.

And she had been right.

If it hadn't been for her routine, Julia was certain that the act of setting her goals and dreams aside would have crushed her spirit so badly she wouldn't have been able to function and come through for her parents the way she had. She had taken everything over, becoming what her mother was quick to point out was not just her right hand, but her left one, as well.

Julia owed that to a well-instilled sense of structure, not to mention to a very keen sense of family loyalty.

"Your father," Annie said, answering her question, "is the same as he was yesterday and, God willing, the

same as he will be tomorrow. Well, but not perfect."
She paused to smile at her daughter. "But then, no man
is ever perfect."

It was a familiar mantra that her mother had uttered
more than a handful of times.

What was different this time was the sadness around
the edges of her smile. And the deeper sadness she
could see in her mother's eyes.

Taking the straw broom out of her mother's hands,
Julia leaned it against the closest wall. She then took
both of her mother's hands in hers and said, "Mom, if
your face was hanging down any lower, you wouldn't
need that broom to sweep up all that imaginary dust
you always see on the floor. You could use your chin.
Now come clean. What's wrong?"

Annie took a breath, apparently struggling to find
the right words.

"It's you."

Julia stared at her mother. Whatever she'd expected
to hear, it wasn't that.

"Me?" she cried incredulously.

Her mother's answer had succeeded in stunning her.
How could she possibly be responsible for that look of
utter devastation on her mother's remarkably unlined
face? Hadn't she all but lived and breathed family and
the business for twelve years now, leaving aside her
own hopes and dreams?

In her view, that would have been cause for her
mother to celebrate, not look as if someone precious
to her had just died.

"Mom, how can you say that? What more can I do?

I'm almost knocking myself out every day to make sure the store stays open and running," Julia pointed out.

Her mother shook her head, her expression telling her that she just didn't understand. "That's just it, Julia. You *shouldn't* have to be knocking yourself out. This is the time of your life that you should look back on fondly when you get to be my age. You shouldn't be forced to feel like you worked your life away."

"But I *don't* feel that way, Mom," Julia protested with feeling. Granted, there were times when she felt as if she did nothing *but* work, but for the most part, she did fine running the grocery store—not to mention putting out her baked goods in a little area that was set aside for the shopper who required a cup of coffee and a pastry to jump-start their morning.

Rather than look relieved, her mother looked as if she was growing agitated for her.

"Well, if you don't, you should," her mother insisted. "You should be resentful that your father and I stole twelve perfectly good years of your life away from you by allowing you to be here for us."

Still holding her mother's hands, Julia led her to a chair over in the corner, just behind the main counter, and knelt in front of her, looking directly into her mother's kind, warm eyes.

"Mom, what's this all about?" she asked gently.

"Maybe I'm seeing things clearly for the first time in years. This isn't fair to you, honey," she insisted, "making you work here day after day. You've sacrificed your education, your career, your marriage—"

"Hold it," Julia declared, holding up her hand. "Back

it up, Mom. First of all, I didn't sacrifice my education. I can always go back to college. It would take a little doing, but it's not impossible. Second, I do that. I can get a career going. And besides, the one I had my eye on back then didn't ultimately require having a college degree so much as it required dedication—it still does," she said, unlocking the front door, then walking back to her mother.

"And third, working here was not what killed my marriage. Mutual, soul-snuffing boredom did that." Julia sighed, feeling a wave of sadness taking root. She had never failed at anything before, but it was about time she accepted the fact that she'd failed at marriage. "Neal and I should have never gotten married in the first place."

"But Neal was such a nice boy," Annie pointed out, protesting the whole idea that their marriage had been a mistake from the beginning.

"Yes, he was and he still is," Julia readily agreed. "But we got married because it seemed like the right thing to do and *nobody* should get married thinking pragmatically like that. When Neal and I were married, there was no magic, no chemistry, no starbursts—and those are three *very* important qualities to have in the foundation of a marriage," Julia stressed.

Leaning in, Julia affectionately pressed a kiss to her mother's forehead. "So stop beating yourself up. I'm exactly where I'm supposed to be and when the time is right, I'll go on to another phase of my life. Until then," she said, rising to her feet again, "why don't you make

sure all the eggs are out of the refrigerator in the stor-
age room?"

The bell that hung over the entrance to the grocery
store rang, signaling the arrival of the store's first customer of the day.

"You do that," she told her mother, "while I go see
what this customer wants."

Turning from her mother, Julia found herself looking
straight up at Liam Jones. She wasn't a short woman—
five foot eight in her bare feet and her feet weren't
bare—but at six foot three Liam literally seemed to
tower over her. Especially, she noted, since he was
wearing boots that added another inch and a half to
his height.

Seeing him here surprised her—when was the last
time he'd come to the grocery store?—but Julia managed to recover quickly enough.

"Wow, twice in one week," she joked, referring to
seeing him. "Are the planets about to collide or something equally as dire?"

Liam was frowning. She was beginning to think that
his face had set that way, like some grumpy old man
who whiled away his days parked in a chair on a front
porch, scowling at the world.

"I don't know about the planets, but we sure are,"
he told her darkly.

"And exactly what is *that* supposed to mean?" Julia
wanted to know.

"I came to hear you say that it's not true."

"Okay," Julia said obligingly. "'It's not true.'" She

waited for him to say something. When he didn't, she gave in and asked, "What's not true?"

"The rumors I heard."

They were back to this again, she thought, frustrated. "Okay, I'll bite. *What* rumors?" she asked, gritting her teeth.

What was it about this pompous cowboy that set her so completely on edge every time they were within ten feet of each other?

She couldn't answer that, which only made the whole situation that much more frustrating for her.

"The rumors that say you're trying to convince those damn Fortunes to stick their noses where they don't belong and open up some high-falutin' restaurant in Horseback Hollow."

Now how did he know she'd been talking to the Mendozas?

"'Damn Fortunes'?" she echoed. "Correct me if I'm wrong, but aren't *you* a Fortune?" she challenged.

His sharp, penetrating blue eyes narrowed as he said, "Consider yourself corrected."

That caught her off guard for a second. Had the stories she'd heard been wrong? "So you're *not* a Fortune?"

"No." He all but spit the word out with all the contempt he could put into the two-letter word.

And then she remembered something else she'd heard. Something that completely negated what he'd just told her. "Funny, your mother was in here the other day and she seems to think that all of her children have now adopted the Fortune name." She had him there, Julia thought.

To her surprise, Liam didn't take back his statement. Instead he said, "My mother is too softhearted for her own good. She'll believe anyone. And don't try to turn this thing around so I lose track of the question. Are you or are you not trying to talk those people into bringing their tainted business into our town?"

She seized the word—but not the one he would have thought of.

"That's right, Liam. *Our* town. Not your town, but *our* town. That means I get a say in what happens here, too, not just you and your incredibly narrow vision." The man was practically medieval in his outlook. If it were up to him, everyone would still be living in the dark ages.

Liam looked at her coldly. "So it's true."

She might as well spell it out for him, otherwise she had a feeling that she would have no peace from this man. Why was he so against progress, anyway?

"If you mean am I trying to show Wendy and Marcos Mendoza that building another one of their restaurants here in Horseback Hollow is a very good idea, then yes, it's true." The restaurant would attract business and provide jobs. There was no downside to that.

He succeeded in taking her breath away with his very next question. "Why do you want to destroy the town, Julia?"

For a second she was so stunned she was speechless. And then she found her tongue. "Are you crazy? This wouldn't destroy the town. This would be an incredibly *good* thing for the town."

"Right," Liam sneered. "'A good thing,'" he echoed contemptuously. "And after they build this restaurant, what's next? Bring in chain retail stores? Or maybe a shopping mall? Don't forget, they bring in a chain store, that'll be the end of this little family store of yours, as well." He gestured around the store. "You and your parents will be out living on the street—and you'll have no one to blame but yourself."

How could he come up with all this and still keep a straight face? It was just beyond her. "You know," she told him, "you should really be a science-fiction writer with that imagination of yours."

Annie Tierney picked this moment to emerge out of the rear storeroom. Seeing Liam beside her daughter, the woman beamed and came forward.

"Hello, Liam," she greeted him. "Tell me, how is your mother feeling these days?"

Chapter Three

Annie Tierney's unannounced appearance caught Liam off guard.

He offered her a polite smile. "She's feeling fine, Mrs. Tierney."

Julia's mother laughed, the look on her face telling him that he had misunderstood her question. "I'm not asking after her health, dear. I'm asking how she feels about finding out that she's actually the long-lost daughter of such a very well-to-do, powerful family. The Fortunes," she added when Jeanne Marie's son didn't immediately respond. "Personally, I find it all very exciting," Annie went on to confide. "It certainly would be a load off my mind if I found out that I was related to them."

The older woman turned to look at her daughter.

There was unmistakable affection in her eyes. "The first thing I'd do is send my girl off to the very best college that money could buy instead of letting her slave her life away here."

"I'm not slaving, Mom," Julia reiterated the point she'd made before Liam had burst into her store with his annoying accusations. "And this is a conversation we can continue later, when we're *alone*." She deliberately emphasized, then looked directly at Liam. "Which will be soon because Liam's just leaving. Aren't you, Liam?" Julia asked, looking at him pointedly as she did her best to muster the semblance of a friendly smile, strictly for her mother's benefit.

"Yeah, I guess I am," he agreed, his eyes never leaving hers, "seeing as how I was never any good at banging my head against a brick wall."

"Oh, you poor dear," Annie declared, instantly sympathetic. As she spoke, Annie reached up to move Liam's light brown hair off his forehead so she could examine it, but he took a step back, preventing her.

"No, ma'am, don't worry. I didn't hit my head in your store."

When Annie looked at him quizzically, Liam knew she was waiting for him to explain his comment. He was forced to lie so that the woman wouldn't think he was being flippant about the Superette. He really liked Annie Tierney. She was friendly, always saw the good in everyone and had a kind soul. In his opinion, Julia could have stood to learn a few things from her mother.

"Then where did you hit your head?" Annie asked.

"At the ranch," he told her, trying to ease away from

the topic. "Last week," he added to forestall any further questions.

"Oh, well mind you watch yourself," Annie cautioned. "Head injuries aren't something to just be shrugged off." And then the serious look on her face vanished as she told him, "I just put on a kettle in the back. Would you care for some tea?"

"No, but thank you for the offer." Since he knew it seemed rather odd that he'd come into the grocery store without buying anything and was now leaving empty-handed, he told the older woman, "I just came by to have a word with your daughter."

"Oh." The thin face lit up, completely erasing the very few lines that were evident. "Well, then by all means, have words," Annie said encouragingly. "Don't mind me. I'll just be in the back, having my tea," she told them as she made her way out of the store and retreated to the storeroom again.

"She's a very nice lady," Liam commented to Julia, watching her mother leave.

Well, there at least he would get no disagreement from her, Julia thought. That was possibly the *only* area that they wouldn't clash over. For the most part, he had the very annoying ability of making her want to say "black" whenever he said "white."

"Yes, she is," Julia agreed quietly, deliberately avoiding making any eye contact with him.

Liam obviously had no such inclination. Instead he turned to look at her. Julia could tell by his expression that the temporary truce that had been silently called while her mother had been in the immediate vicinity was officially over.

"What would she say if she knew?" he suddenly challenged.

Okay, maybe she just wasn't sharp today, Julia thought shortly. What the hell was he talking about now?

"Knew about what?"

He looked at her as if she'd suddenly turned simple. She caught herself wanting to strangle him.

"That you're seriously thinking about trying to get the Fortunes to bring their big-city blight right here to Horseback Hollow."

"If you're still referring to my wanting to encourage Wendy and her husband to open up their second restaurant here, she would probably say, 'Go for it, Julia.'" She raised her chin like someone bracing for a grueling battle. "My mother has always been very supportive of my dreams and I've had this one for a very long time."

His eyes became blue laserlike slits as he regarded her. "So you're telling me that it's your dream to destroy Horseback Hollow?"

She wasn't saying any such thing and he knew it, Julia thought angrily. How could she have *ever* been attracted to this Neanderthal? She must have been out of her mind.

"No," Julia contradicted with feeling, struggling not to raise her voice and yell at him. The last thing she wanted to do was to have her mother overhear her giving Liam a piece of her mind—even if he did sorely need it. But she'd had just about all she could take of his holier-than-thou pontificating. "It's always been my dream to build the town up."

He laughed shortly. "Right now, that's the same thing from where I'm standing."

And just who had died and made him the reigning authority on things like this?

"Well, then, maybe you'd better move and get the sun out of your eyes because you certainly aren't seeing things clearly."

"The town's doing just fine as it is," he insisted. What was wrong with her? "Why can't you see how destructive it would be to allow outsiders' interests to take over Horseback Hollow? What do we need with another restaurant, anyway?" he challenged her.

Just how blind was he? she wondered, frustrated. "Does the term 'freedom of choice' *mean* anything to you?" she returned frostily.

His mouth curved in a humorless smile. "Only if it means I'm free to ignore you."

"Go right ahead," she declared, gesturing toward the door. "But you're going to have to do it outside my store."

The next moment she'd suddenly put her hands against his back and began to push him toward the door.

She managed to move Liam a few stumbling feet only because she'd caught him by surprise. But once he regained his balance, Liam employed his full weight as a counterforce and there was no way she could budge him more than a couple of shaky inches.

"I just want to say one more thing—" he began.

Exhausted by her effort to move him any farther

toward the door, Julia dropped her hands to her sides. "I'll hold you to that," she told him sharply.

"How are your folks going to feel when this store is forced to close down?" His tone was surprisingly mild as he put the question to her. He looked like a man who felt he'd scored his winning goal and was just waiting for the fact to sink in with the opposing team.

Julia, however, looked at him as if she thought he'd just lost his mind.

"Why would this store be forced to close down?" She wanted to know his rationale.

Like a parent introducing a new concept to a child, he began to patiently explain. "Hey, chain drugstores aren't going to be the only thing that'll be turning up here once you open the floodgates and start 'building the town up.' Big chain supermarkets will be horning their way in here, too." Liam paused to look around the grocery store that had remained relatively unchanged for most of his lifetime. He found that rather comfortingly reassuring. "And this store, with its neat little aisles and limited selections will be boarded up faster than you can say 'I told you so,'" he concluded.

"I wouldn't be saying 'I told you so.'" There were small, sharp daggers coming from her eyes, all aimed at his heart—if he actually *had* one. "That would be your line," she retorted.

"Yes," Liam agreed, grinning from ear to ear. "It would be."

The strange thing about that grin, Julia later recalled, was that it didn't seem to reach his eyes. In her experience, any smile or grin that was genuine in scope always included the eyes. Without the eyes being involved, the person who was smiling was only trying to fool people as to his mind-set.

Sometimes, she couldn't help thinking, they were out to fool themselves, as well. The first time she noticed the difference between real smiles and ones that were entrenched in deception, consciously or otherwise, was when she'd caught a glimpse of her own face in the mirror on her wedding day.

Her eyes hadn't been smiling then, either. At the time, she was doing what she felt was the "right thing." It had taken her three years before she'd admitted that to herself.

"Look," she told Liam, "either buy something or leave. I've got work to do and I don't have time to let you go on badgering me like this because you're so small-minded you can't see that you either progress or wither and die on the vine. And *you* might be content to let Horseback Hollow stagnate, but I want it to flourish."

He looked at her for a long moment, as if he was debating saying anything to her or not. Finally he said, "There's a third alternative in that multiple choice of yours."

She didn't see it and couldn't imagine what his point was. "Enlighten me," she told him.

He laughed at her choice of words. "That'll take a lot longer than I have right now. But let me just tell you what that third choice is…. It's maintaining the status quo."

That was just theme and variation of one of the two choices she'd presented to him.

"In other words, stagnating," she declared. But before he could say anything further to contradict what he'd just labeled his so-called "third" choice, Julia started talking rapidly to get her point across.

"Nothing ever remains the same, no matter how much you might want it to. Change is inevitable and you can't stop it or stand in its way. But you *can* guide it," she emphasized.

Liam frowned as he shook his head, the ultimate immovable object to her irresistible force. "Sorry, it's going to take a hell of a lot more than that to convince me to surrender to the boys with the deep pockets. I'd rather just go my own way."

"Why don't you?" she said encouragingly. The next moment she'd crossed the floor to the door and held it wide open for him, her meaning clear. "Nobody here will stop you, that's for damn sure."

Rather than do exactly that and just leave, Liam pulled himself up to his full height and seemed to just loom over her, his bearing fully emphasizing just how much taller than her he really was.

"No, but someone should really stop you," he told her in a voice that was completely devoid of any humor. "Before it's too late and we all wind up suffering the consequences."

Again Julia raised her chin defiantly, her eyes flashing as she barely managed to suppress her anger.

"It'll take a better man than you to do it," she informed him hotly.

"Maybe," Liam allowed, "but that doesn't mean I can't try."

Before Julia could ask him just what he intended to do, Liam did it.

Did something he hadn't even foreseen himself doing—at least not in the heat of this exchange. Although if he were being completely honest with himself, he would have had to admit that he *had* envisioned *exactly* this transpiring more than just once or twice in his head—as well as in his unguarded dreams.

One second they were exchanging glares and hot words, the next it was no longer just the words that were hot.

It was the two of them.

Liam had caught her by her shoulders and brought his mouth down on hers.

There was the argument that doing this was the *only* way to stop her from talking and, more importantly, from espousing the so-called cause she seemed so intent on pushing.

There was a whole host of arguments and half-truths he could have told himself about why he had done what he'd done. But deep in his soul, he knew that there was only one real reason he was doing this.

Because he wanted to.

Rather than embracing the cause that was so close to her heart, after a beat, to her dismay, Julia found herself embracing *him* instead. Found herself weaving her arms around Liam's neck as best she could, raising herself up on her tiptoes so that she could lean her body into his.

She *had* to have lost her mind; there was no other explanation for behaving this way.

Yet, as upset as doing this made her, Julia just could *not* make herself pull back or break away from Liam and his lethal lips.

Not even the tiniest bit.

Not when the very blood in her veins was rising to an alarming temperature and the room was spinning around her faster than Dorothy's house when it was snatched up by the twister that had sent it whisking off to Oz.

Julia realized that her heart rate had quickened to the point of doubling and the very air seemed to have disappeared right out of her lungs.

Heaven knew that she'd been kissed before, more times than she could possibly count. And of course she'd made love before, as well, but this... This was some kind of new, crazy sensation that she had never, *ever* encountered before and although she knew, *knew* in her heart, that whatever this was, was bad for her, she just couldn't make herself pull away and stop.

Not yet.

A few seconds from now, yes, but *not yet*.

Liam was completely convinced that he had succeeded in utterly losing his mind. There was no other reason for what was going on.

He wasn't that eighteen-year-old hotshot that he had once been anymore, wasn't that cocky high school senior who reveled in the adulation he saw in every single high school girl's eyes when she looked at him.

Back then, he'd thrived on those looks and those girls.

But right now he would have been hard-pressed to remember *any* of their names. They all seemed like just so many interchangeable entities, feeding his fragile young ego and providing a release for all those wild, raging hormones that plagued so many boys at that age.

He'd eventually outgrown that stage, settled down in his thinking and while he did enjoy female companionship with a fair amount of regularity, he wasn't looking for anything permanent because he wasn't interested in settling down with any one woman.

Settling.

There wasn't really a single girl he'd gone out with, a single girl or woman in Horseback Hollow who turned up in his dreams at night, who gave him a reason to whistle tunelessly to himself as he looked forward to Saturday-night outings.

But this, whatever *this* was, was different. Different enough to put a fire in his belly and make him suddenly feel alive.

Finally pulling back—because Liam was afraid that if he didn't, he wouldn't be able to surface ever again— he looked at the woman who had just shaken up the foundations of his well-ordered world. Looked at her for a long, hard moment.

And when he spoke, the words could definitely not be viewed as romantic in any manner, shape or form.

"What the hell was that?" He wanted to know.

"I have no idea," Julia answered hoarsely, trying desperately to look angry, to *feel* angry, and completely unable to manage to do either. "But don't ever do it again."

"Don't worry, I won't," Liam replied in a voice that

was just as hoarse as hers, a fact that really annoyed him no end.

He said it because, at the time, he meant it.

Or at least he *thought* he did.

Chapter Four

Harlan Osgood wore not one but two hats in his everyday life.

First and foremost, like his father before him, Harlan was the town barber. He owned and ran The Cuttery, Horseback Hollow's only barbershop. Eventually he'd expanded the shop to include a hair salon, as well, for those ladies who were brave enough to cross the threshold and place the fate of their flowing tresses in Harlan's hands.

Almost everyone in town sat in one of his chairs at one time or another, most on a fairly regular basis. Interacting with these town residents gave Harlan some insight into the way the locals felt about all sorts of matters that concerned them. He was a good listener, always had been, and that, in turn, helped him make some of the decisions he needed to make when he donned his other hat, the one that figuratively belonged to the town mayor.

All things considered, the latter was almost an honorary position. For one thing, there was next to no monetary compensation for the job. Being elected mayor by the good people of Horseback Hollow fed his self-esteem rather than helped him put food on the table. That was what running the Cuttery was for.

Harlan had always been considered a decent, fair man by his friends and neighbors. He wasn't one to impose his will over the objection of others, didn't look for ways—devious or otherwise—to line his pockets or the pockets of his friends at the town's expense. What had put Harlan in office and kept him there election after election was his honest belief that in a town as small as Horseback Hollow, that everyone's voice really counted and was equal to everyone else's.

The way he saw it, one person was no better, no worse than another, and that included him.

Harlan first heard the rumor about the possibility of a new restaurant—funded by some of the Fortunes of Red Rock—coming here to Horseback Hollow the way he heard about almost everything else that came to his attention: from one of the customers sitting in his barber's chair.

In less than forty-eight hours, what began as a vague rumor quickly became the topic that was on *everyone's* lips. No matter who was doing the talking, it seemed that everyone, young or old, had an opinion on the subject of this new restaurant that might be coming.

Some spoke with feelings and passion about this restaurant that had yet to materialize. Others chose to feel *him* out first before stating how *they* felt on the matter.

"What do you think about that new place that's coming to Horseback?" Riley Johnson, one of his most regular customers, asked him.

The rancher, lean and rangy of build, came in for a haircut like clockwork every two weeks despite the fact that he had very little hair to speak of these days. He came, Harlan suspected, for the company and a chance for some male interaction. Riley owned a fairly small spread as far as ranches in the area went and he and his wife had been blessed with all girls. Riley spent most of his days feeling outnumbered.

The barbershop was a place to regroup.

Riley twisted around in his chair to look at the man he'd known going on five decades, waiting for the latter to answer.

"Well, it's not a done deal just yet, Riley," Harlan pointed out as he made rhythmic cuts to the hair that *was* there.

"I heard it's more done than not," Clyde Hanks, another regular, waiting for his turn with Harlan, spoke up.

"Well, you heard wrong," Harlan told him, keeping his eyes on his work and Riley's balding pate. "Nobody's put in any papers for it and nothing's crossed my desk yet. There's gotta be permits issued, land measured, all sorts of tedious things like that before anything gets started," Harlan said. "You boys know that."

Riley still looked a bit skeptical. "And you're not just holding out on us?"

"No reason not to tell you if it was happening," Harlan answered mildly.

"You ask me, it's not a good idea," Riley said.

"Bringing in new business is *always* a good idea," Clyde maintained.

Harlan could see both sides of the matter, the way he always did. The good *and* the bad. Which was why he decided that calling a town meeting to put the matter up for discussion and then eventually to a vote might just be the best way to handle this budding tempest in a teapot—before that teapot boiled over.

The meeting was set for Friday evening at seven.

As always, Harlan relied primarily on word of mouth to spread the news of the town meeting. To play it safe, he also had a couple of notices posted, one in the Superette because most of the town frequented the grocery store, and one in the town's only post office. To his way of thinking, this was as close to covering all bases as he could possibly get.

And then Harlan went back to business as usual, doing what needed to be done until the day of the meeting.

Julia glanced at her watch. It was almost time for the meeting. She was so preoccupied, going over what she wanted to say and trying very hard not to be nervous, that she didn't hear her father's soft footfalls until he was next to her. The once heavyset man had lost a great deal of weight, but he was on the mend and determined to get better with each passing day.

"Julia?"

"Oh, Dad, you scared me," she said, looking up, startled.

He smiled at her. "I just wanted to wish you luck tonight. Some of our friends and neighbors can be real stubborn about changing anything." His protective attitude toward her was out in full display as he said, "Maybe I should go with you."

He still thought of himself as being stronger than he was. She knew these baby steps toward full recovery were frustrating for him, but she didn't want him taking on more than he should. "No, you know excitement isn't good for you, Dad. You've more than done enough already," she told him with feeling. "Finding out about the Mendozas and how they were looking for a new location for a second restaurant, setting up my introduction to them… I'll take it from here."

"You know, I wanted this for you. Wanted to find some way to pay you back for what you gave up to stay here for me."

She didn't want him to feel obliged to her in any way. She'd stayed out of love, not because anyone had made her. "Dad—"

"Let me have my say, Julie. I didn't do all that much, just asked around to find out where you could get in contact with that Marcos Mendoza guy. Most of it was just a matter of luck, anyway, him being married to Wendy Fortune. They're looking to expand their business, so why shouldn't it be here? Especially since

James Fortune is so thrilled to finally make contact with his long-lost sister Jeanne Marie, and her living right here in Horseback Hollow. You might even call it fate. I just tugged a little on fate's hand, that's all. You did the rest. You wrote to them and laid it all out, nice and pretty, the way I knew you would, telling them about all the ways building their next restaurant right here was a good idea for them *and* for the town. You always did have a real good head on your shoulders, Julie. Almost as good as your heart," he said with barely contained emotion.

Moved, she hugged him. "I love you, Dad."

"Right back at you, baby. Now go knock 'em dead," he urged.

The meeting was held at the Two Moon Saloon. As usual, the bar was declared officially closed for the duration of the meeting. The establishment's tables were all pushed to the side, against the walls, and extra folding chairs had been brought in.

As always, there were more people than chairs, but that was just the way things were and no one seemed to mind all that much. Standing for the duration of the meeting seemed like a small price to pay for being included in the town's voting process.

At exactly the stroke of seven, Harlan began the meeting. "Thank you all for coming," he said, addressing people he considered to be his friends rather than his constituents. "I don't think many of you have to be told why we're here."

"I dunno about anyone else, but I'm here to get out of

doing more chores," a male voice at the back of the room piped up. A smattering of laughter followed the remark.

"Glad we could help you out, Zack," Harlan said, recognizing the speaker's voice. "All right, let's get started," he declared, bringing down his gavel and officially calling the meeting to order. "It's recently come to my attention that there's been some serious talk about some out-of-towners thinking of opening up a new restaurant right here in town."

"Why do we need another restaurant? What's wrong with The Grill, I'd like to know?" a woman on the left asked indignantly.

"Have you been there lately? It ain't exactly the Four Seasons," her neighbor, a woman with a rather heavy-set face, pointed out.

"Well, this ain't exactly New York now, is it?" the first woman countered.

"Ladies, ladies, you'll all get your chance to state your opinions," Harlan promised calmly. "That's why we're here. No need to try to shout one another down. We're not taking a final vote tonight. That's for the next meeting. Right now, we're just going to discuss it. All right, one at a time, please," he requested, looking out at the sea of faces before him. "Who wants to go first to make a case for or against a new restaurant opening up in Horseback Hollow?"

More than a few hands shot up. This certainly was a hot topic, Harlan thought. He fervently hoped that it wouldn't divide the town and put the residents at odds with one another. Something like that could turn ugly quickly.

Though he rarely expressed his own opinion on things, he felt strongly about one thing. He would not stand by and see the people who were his neighbors come to blows over this. He wouldn't allow the restaurant to be built here if it came down to that.

Though she was friendly on a one-to-one basis, especially with her store's customers, for the most part Julia considered herself to be rather on the shy side. She certainly didn't like to call attention to herself, and as a rule, didn't like speaking up in a crowded room. She always preferred to keep out of the spotlight.

Julia had attended more than one town meeting without saying a single word during the proceedings, only raising her hand those times when a vote had to be taken.

But this was different.

This—the restaurant that was under discussion—could very well mean the resurrection of her own dream, as well as representing some definite choices for the residents of Horseback Hollow.

Contemplating the restaurant's advent, Julia had already gone so far as to create whole menus in her head, menus that offered *so* much more than The Grill—the building next to the saloon—did. The latter only served burgers, hot dogs and a grilled-cheese sandwich, which served as the establishment's main and most popular meal. The selection at The Grill was so limited that it almost hurt.

So, after listening to one opinion being stated after another, with little being resolved—it was more like

mundane bickering—Julia decided that maybe it was
time for her to speak up on the side of the restaurant.
She could see only pluses in having the business built
here.

"Anyone else want to say something?" Harlan asked
when the last speaker had finally and mercifully run out
of steam and sat down. His eyes quickly swept the room.

When he saw the raised hand, he looked rather surprised to see who that hand belonged to.

"Julia?" he said uncertainly. "Would you like to say
something?" Even as he asked, the mayor still expected
to hear her say "No," that she hadn't really meant to
raise her hand.

But she didn't.

"Yes, Mr. Mayor, I would," she said in a firm voice
that gave no hint to the fact that her stomach had flipped
over and was currently tied up in a very tight knot.

"Well, stand up and speak up," he said, gesturing
for her to rise. "No use talking if nobody can hear you
or see you."

"Might not be any use her talking even if we can,"
someone scoffed.

"Shut up, Silas, and let her say her piece."

The tersely worded command didn't come from the
mayor, as Julia might have expected. It had come from
Liam Jones.

Stunned, she looked over toward where the rancher
was standing at the back of the room. He was indolently
leaning against a wall, the expression on his face mod-
erately contemptuous. Initially, she would have said the
contempt was aimed at her. But now, with his becom-

ing her unlikely defender, she really couldn't say *what* Liam was being so contemptuous of.

"Thank you," she mouthed.

Liam just nodded silently in response, indicated that she should get on with what she had to say.

Liam Jones was a hard man to read, Julia thought, turning her attention back to the subject that had brought her here.

In truth, Liam wasn't sure just what had prompted him to speak up just now to silence the would-be heckler. The man had only said aloud what he himself had been thinking. But the thought of someone trying to ridicule Julia into holding her peace had unexpectedly raised a fire in his belly.

If anyone was going to put her in her place, it was going to be *him,* not some half-wit who thought himself to be clever. And he definitely didn't want to hear her put in her place in front of a crowd where she could be publicly humiliated. There was no call for that sort of crude behavior.

Julia's soft, melodic voice broke into his train of thought. Liam turned his attention, albeit somewhat against his will, toward the redhead who had been haunting his thoughts ever since he'd kissed her and had messed up life as he knew it.

"Now I know that a lot of you think that things are going along just fine the way they are in Horseback Hollow—" A smattering of voices agreeing with her echoed around the room. "But they're not really," Julia insisted. The same voices now muttered protests.

Harlan raised his gavel in a warning gesture as he looked around the room, daring the mumblers to continue. The murmurings stopped.

Julia continued as if nothing had happened. "You can't tell me that things are so good, so perfect that we couldn't stand to have a little more revenue coming into the town."

"You mean like taxes?" someone asked, somewhat confused as to where she was going with this.

"No," Julia answered patiently. "I mean like people coming here from some of the nearby towns to eat at the new restaurant and spend their money."

"So the people who own the restaurant make money, what's that do for us?" Riley Johnson challenged. Julia could see by the man's expression that he was one of the ones she needed to convert to her way of thinking. The man could be very persuasive when he spoke.

"What it means to us is a great deal," Julia insisted, quickly explaining, "after all, the restaurant isn't going to run itself. It's going to need waitresses and busboys as well as people to do the cooking, to make sure there's enough food, enough coffee, tea and other beverages to drink. It takes a lot to run a decent-size restaurant.

"The restaurant's backers are going to be hiring local people, not busing in people regularly from Red Rock," she pointed out, effectively shooting down a rumor she'd heard making the rounds this morning. "And those customers who'll come to eat at the restaurant, they're not just all going to get back into their cars and drive away into the night," she said with a laugh. "Maybe they'll stay and look around, buy something before they go—"

"The town's only got a handful of shops," Riley pointed out, still not convinced that the good outweighed what he viewed as the bad in this case.

Julia approached the subject from another angle. "Maybe this'll encourage some of you to open up more stores. The way it is right now, we have to drive to other towns to get almost everything. For example, we could stand to have a full-size bakery right here in Horseback Hollow," she suggested.

Liam raised his voice above the voices of several other people, pointing out, "You've got a bakery in your store."

"What we've got are doughnuts and coffee," Julia corrected him, smiling amicably. "I'm talking about a *real* bakery, one that has proper cakes, pies, fresh-baked bread straight out of the oven on the premises, to name just a few things."

She looked around to see if she was getting through and to her surprise, she began to make out faces rather than just a sea of blurred features and hair all running together.

Some of those faces were smiling at her with encouragement. Julia took heart in that.

"I'm talking about building up a place that I am proud to call home. It is *not* going to be easy and it is not going to happen overnight. But it all starts with that first step," she said with sincerity because she really believed what she was telling the people at the meeting.

Unconsciously holding her breath, she looked around the room to see if she had managed to make her neighbors understand.

"Yeah, but that 'step' you're talking about involves inviting those Fortunes into our town," someone toward the back piped up. "Who knows, after they're finished, it might not even *be* our town any longer."

Where did they get these ideas? Julia couldn't help wondering. Even as she did, she caught herself slanting a look in Liam's direction.

Had *he* started that baseless rumor? She didn't want to think that and he *had* come to her defense when Silas Marshall had tried to heckle her, but Liam wasn't the kind of man who could be easily swayed with just a few well-placed words and a smile. The man was nothing if not frustratingly stubborn.

"Now listen," she said. "I've done some research on the subject of the Fortunes. I found out that this family *always* gives back to the community they're in, usually far more than they ever received. Why, they even built a medical clinic in Red Rock and started the Fortune Foundation."

"What's that?" Dinah Jackson queried.

"That's a nonprofit, charitable organization that helps take care of people in need," Julia answered, addressing her words to the woman directly. "People who might have fallen on hard times through no fault of their own."

"Oh, handouts," someone snorted contemptuously.

At times, these people had more pride than sense, Julia couldn't help thinking.

"No, a hand *up*." She put emphasis on the last word. There was a difference. "The foundation helps people stand up on their own two feet again. As far as I can see, there's nothing wrong with that."

A smattering of murmurings rose around the room again as people made comments to their neighbors, rendering their own opinions on what seemed to be the Fortunes' obviously selfless behavior.

There were a few in the gathering who required more convincing—Liam among them—but for the most part, Julia could see that she had managed get the wavering and undecided thinking about the benefits of having this new restaurant here.

The mayor scanned the room, took note of some of the expressions and made a judgment call.

"All right, I think that we've had a fair amount of pro and con debating on this subject for tonight. It's getting kind of late and we all have somewhere to be. If there are no objections, why don't we put the matter to a preliminary vote, see where we all stand on this issue right now? Remember," he warned, "no matter what the outcome of tonight's vote is, nothing's final. You all have time to think about this, do a little research before we take a final vote on the matter. As of right now, there've been no concrete bids made yet, no proposals about building this restaurant.

"As far as I know, this could just be one great big rumor with legs," Harlan told the people at the meeting, chuckling at the verbal image he had just created for them.

"If the preliminary vote turns out to be yes, then I will personally go to Marcos and Wendy Mendoza and convince them to build their second restaurant right here in the heart of Horseback Hollow," Julia promised.

The "heart" of Horseback, at the moment, only involved a two-block radius since that was all that actually comprised the little town.

"Mendoza?" Clyde Hanks echoed, confused. "I thought you said that the Fortunes were the ones who were behind this venture. Just who the heck are Marcos and Wendy Mendoza?" He, as did many others, wanted to know.

"Her name's Wendy *Fortune* Mendoza," Liam told the man tersely.

It felt as though everywhere he turned, he just couldn't get away and avoid those damn people, Liam thought darkly. They were trying to worm their way into his family and now into his town. Maybe the first was happening because they wanted the latter, he realized.

The Fortunes were like some biblical plague he couldn't outrun.

Chapter Five

"Bet you're pretty proud of yourself, aren't you?" Liam remarked, his tone of voice completely unreadable.

Coming out of the saloon at the end of the town meeting, Julia was utterly preoccupied, her mind rushing around here and there as she made plans to get in touch with the Mendozas first thing in the morning. Though nothing had been finalized between them, she was very hopeful that if and when the restaurant did come here, she could impress them enough with her skills to be hired as at least one of the chefs. To that end, she wanted to keep them abreast of what was happening as far as the town's considering the possibility of voting to have the restaurant built in Horseback Hollow.

The preliminary vote regarding the restaurant's construction on Horseback soil had been close, very close, but it looked as if more people were for it than against it. That, in turn, made Julia very excited. She intended to try to bring *everyone* around by the time the final vote was taken.

This was the beginning, she could *feel* it.

Lost in thought, she didn't see Liam standing adjacent to the saloon's entrance, leaning against the side of the building. Busy making plans, she wasn't aware of him at all until he spoke. She'd very nearly jumped out of her skin. She'd thought he'd be halfway home by now, especially since he'd walked out after the vote was tallied and it was obvious that the position he'd taken wasn't going to win. At least, not tonight.

To Liam, the fact that the vote had been so extremely close made the very real possibility of an ultimate loss all the more painful to him. It was one of those "so near and yet so far" moments.

Regaining her composure and managing to cover up the flustered feeling that had corkscrewed through her without warning at the sound of Liam's voice, Julia squared her shoulders as she resumed walking back to the Superette. The grocery store would be open for another half hour because of the meeting and she needed to get back. Tonight her mother was manning the register alone and she didn't want her to be too taxed.

"Yes, I am, actually," she said, responding to the flippant assumption he had tossed at her. She'd said it in as cheerful a tone as she could.

Because she had a natural tendency to want to see everyone happy, she decided to give raising Liam's spirits a shot. "The new restaurant is going to be a good thing for the town, you'll see," she promised him.

"Maybe you and I have a different definition of 'good thing,'" he pointed out with a trace of barely suppressed sarcasm.

"My definition involves prosperity," she replied succinctly.

They'd already gone all through this at the meeting. Hadn't he been paying attention? Why was he refusing to give the whole venture a chance? What was he *really* afraid of? she couldn't help wondering.

His eyes pinned her down, almost keeping her a prisoner as he stated his feelings about the fate of the town. "Mine has to do with the town keeping its individuality, in not turning its back on its roots just to put a few pieces of silver into a few people's pockets."

He made it sound as if she was trying to get the people of Horseback Hollow to sell out for her own private gain and she deeply resented his implication. Selling out had absolutely nothing to do with this.

"People don't deal in silver anymore, Liam," she informed him tersely. "It's the twenty-first century, not the 1850s."

He regarded her for a long, poignant moment, his thoughts utterly masked behind an expressionless face. "Maybe that's the problem," he told her.

She was *not* going to get sucked into playing any mind games. "Maybe the problem is that you're a dream killer," she accused angrily.

Couldn't he see past his own dislike of the Fortunes long enough to try to understand what the infusion of new blood, new places could do for the town, for its economy? How it could just lift up everyone's lifestyle at least a notch or two?

"The 'dream' is the simple life we have here and you're the one killing it because you're an opportunist," he accused, his temper suddenly flaring higher—more than the situation warranted. "Look, aside from all my other objections, I just don't think it's really smart to invite more of these people into Horseback Hollow. Just look what happened with that pilot, Orlando. You going to tell me what happened to him in his plane was just an accident? Not to mention that there've been a bunch of anonymous flyers showing up at the post office here, saying Fortunes Go Home! Can't be any clearer than that."

"Orlando's not a Fortune. He's a Mendoza," Julia began, but got no further.

"A Mendoza who was piloting a plane for Sawyer Fortune. He almost got killed when it malfunctioned. These people are bad news. I say pack it up and go back to where you came from, don't give them another reason to set up camp."

He could see that he just wasn't getting through to her and it exasperated him. They were standing all but toe-to-toe right now. "You think just because you kissed me the other day I'm going to wag my tail and meekly follow you no matter what?"

Her eyes widened in utter shock. How *could* he say that?

"Hold it, buster," she ordered angrily. "I think you

have your facts a little mixed up. *I* didn't kiss *you*," Julia reminded him flatly. "*You* were the one who kissed *me*."

Liam shrugged as if he hadn't really expected her to say anything else about the matter. Her denial left him completely unfazed. "If it makes you feel better to believe that, go right ahead," he told her in a disinterested voice.

She hated how he twisted things. "It's not a matter of 'believing' it, it's what happened," Julia insisted, her eyes narrowing as she silently dared him to actually deny it.

There went that chin of hers again, he noted, watching as it stuck up pugnaciously. The single action gave him such a tempting target that he found himself having a really hard time resisting it.

But a man never hit a lady—not unless he was fighting for his life and although that might be what was going on figuratively, in reality it was just a heated battle of words

And even though in their own way those words could deliver even heavier blows to the heart and psyche than fists could, he was *not* about to give Julia the satisfaction of glimpsing that tender region that belonged to him and him alone.

"Looks like we're not going to agree on that, either," he observed.

Had there not been the very real possibility that one of the people who had attended the meeting could stumble over them right now, he would have swept Julia into his arms and showed her what being kissed by him actually meant and felt like.

But, like his father, Liam had always been a very private man. He had absolutely no desire to become the focal point for local gossips. Since the possible construction of this outsider-backed restaurant had everyone stirred up, one way or another, this little drama currently unfolding between Julia and him would be like throwing kindling into a campfire that was already lit.

They would be irresistible fodder for the tongue-waggers of this town and beyond. He wanted no part of that.

So, throwing up his hands, Liam made an unintelligible sound and stormed away before he and Julia could get deeply embroiled in yet *another* argument.

Unlike Julia and more than half the people in that damn saloon who voted with her, Liam thought as he kept walking, he could *not* see anything good coming of this venture Julia was so hot about. What it was going to do was change life in Horseback Hollow as they all knew it. He would bet money on it—and *that* wasn't something he *ever* did lightly. He worked too hard for his money to ever waste it on anything other than what he felt was a *sure* thing.

But the majority—a rather damn *slim* majority at that—had voted to give the project a chance to prove itself as they all gave it a closer inspection. It was up to him to find a way to sink this project before it could actively move forward and become a reality. He needed to do something to get the town to vote against it when the final vote was taken.

At the moment, as he cast around, he was coming up empty.

However, he wouldn't have been his father's son, he thought with a hint of a smile curving his mouth, if he just gave up altogether. He was going to have to think on it awhile, like a dog gnawing on a bone. There *had* to be another way to make Julia see reason about this— and he had to find that way *before* the restaurant opened up and eventually ruined the face of the town.

Even if construction started—and no matter which way you sliced it, that was still a ways off—it could be stopped if enough people could be convinced that he was right and she was wrong.

It had come down to that, he thought. Him against her.

The best way for him to go about that, of course, was to convince *her* that she'd made a mistake. If he did that, the rest would fall neatly into place—and the town would be spared.

But what the hell could he do to make her see that what she was proposing wasn't just a restaurant, it was a whole new change of lifestyle for everyone who lived in and around Horseback Hollow?

So caught up in the dilemma ahead of him, Liam didn't see the tall, rangy rancher until he all but stumbled into him. Stopping short to keep from bodily colliding with the six-foot-tall man, there was an apology on his lips before his eyes and brain focused and engaged one another to identify just who it was that he'd almost walked straight into.

"Hey, sorry, I wasn't looking where I—" *Oh, damn,*

he silently cursed. This was the *last* person he wanted to run into right now.

Quinn Drummond had been at the meeting; he'd taken a seat all the way at the back so that he could observe everyone. Liam doubted the rancher had said two words during the meeting. *And* he had voted for the restaurant. Another reason to avoid the man until he came up with his strategy, Liam thought.

Quinn's solemn face gave way to a small smile. "Liam, just the guy I wanted to see. You got a minute?"

He doubted it was going to be this easy to disengage himself but he gave it a try anyway. "Actually, no, I don't. I was just on my way to see someone—"

"Good, I'll walk with you," Quinn offered, falling into step with him.

"I'm going to be *driving* to see this person. Driving *out of town*." Liam built his lie a piece at a time.

Quinn was nothing if not flexible and accommodating. "All right, I'll just walk you to your truck, then. That'll give me a chance to grab at least a couple of minutes of your time."

Liam was about to say that a couple of minutes wouldn't produce any sort of viable results, but Quinn didn't pause or stop talking long enough to allow him to get the legendary word in edgewise.

"Did you get a chance to find out anything at all about what the inside story on Amelia really is?"

Liam began to scowl. Ordinarily most people would back off at that, but Liam could tell Quinn was desperate. Amelia was obviously haunting the man—he needed *answers* and obviously didn't know where to get them.

"I know you're busy," Quinn continued, "but hell, man, she is part of your family and I thought that maybe you could ask someone who knows her just what—"

Liam abruptly stopped walking and sighed. He'd already tried to ignore the young rancher once before when he'd come at him with questions about the Fortunes. The *British* branch of the Fortune family, for God's sake. What was he supposed to know about any of them? He was trying to avoid them, not lobby for a position as the family's best friend.

Specifically, Quinn had questions concerning Amelia Fortune Chesterfield, whose recent engagement to some guy named James Bannings had been the subject matter of endless headlines, magazine covers and an incredible amount of media coverage that Liam found infinitely boring. There were enough speculations bouncing around about the duo to boggle the average intelligent mind.

In his opinion, the whole thing was just hogwash. Who gave a damn about two people getting married in England, anyway?

"Look, man," Liam began as evenly as he could manage, "I already told you. I don't know anything more than you do. Less probably."

Quinn couldn't bring himself to understand that. "But she's your cousin. Your mother and her mother are sisters—more than sisters," Quinn noted.

He didn't need to rehash what had already been all

but rammed down his throat, thanks to the newspapers, not to mention his own family.

"Something my mother and even this princess's mother didn't know about until like six months ago," Liam pointed out, cutting Quinn off before he got up a full head of steam on the subject and rambled on end-lessly.

Nevertheless, Quinn didn't give up easily. "But still—"

"There is no 'still,'" Liam informed him. "Look, I don't know how to say this any clearer so that you can understand, but those people—all of them, British or otherwise—are *not* my family. They've never *been* my family and they're never going to *be* my family. Do I make myself clear?" he demanded.

Although he was looking into the face of anger, Quinn refused to be put off like that. "But your mother—"

"Is free to do whatever she wants and if she wants to acknowledge these people and pick up so-called 'fam-ily' ties, fine. So be it. But *I* don't and that's *my* choice. Sharing a name doesn't mean a damn thing to me," Liam insisted heatedly.

Who the hell did the Fortunes think they were, he wanted to know, barging into his life like that and think-ing he and his siblings would just turn their backs on what they believed were their roots, to happily pick up the Fortune mantle? Well, not him, by God. Not him.

"It's more than a name," Quinn stubbornly insisted. "It's blood."

"Yeah, well, I don't believe it." Maybe there was

some underhanded reason that these people came crawling out of their fancy woodwork at this time. He hadn't figured that part out yet. All he knew was that he wanted to be left alone and not hounded about these damn people every which way he turned around.

"Look, Quinn, the bottom line is that I don't know anything about these people and I don't *want* to know anything about these people, so you're going to have to ask someone else about them." Normally not a curious person, curiosity got the better of him this time, thanks to Quinn's relentless persistence. "Considering that this princess you're asking about has her picture plastered all over the front pages, what are you trying to find out about her that hasn't already been covered a hundred times over in every means of communication available?"

Quinn sighed, running his hand through his rather longish brown hair. "I guess I'm just trying to find out if it's true."

Well, that didn't clear anything up. "If what's true?" Liam asked.

It pained Quinn to even frame the question. "If she's actually engaged to this guy Bannings."

He'd seen the headlines himself—and he hadn't particularly wanted to know anything at all about these people. "Well, if it's not true, there're going to be an awful lot of reporters and newshounds with egg on their collective faces."

The second the words were out of his mouth, Liam saw the look of absolute misery cross the other rancher's face. What the hell was *that* all about?

"You got a thing for this Princess Amelia or whatever she's calling herself?" Liam ventured.

Rather than answer the question, Quinn said, "She doesn't use any kind of a title.

"Calling her a princess might be something the tabloids enjoy doing, but when Amelia was out here for Sawyer's wedding at New Year's, she told me that she hated being related to the royal family. It meant that she was never alone, always in the public eye, always having her every movement—her every mistake—photographed and forever documented."

Liam shrugged even as an inkling of sympathy stirred within him. He knew that he would have lost his mind if he had these relentless reporters and photographers following him around like that, night and day.

"Yeah, well, the papers aren't paying attention to what she likes or doesn't like. They're doing what sells, which means they're going to go on calling her a princess."

In his heart, Quinn had thought of her as *his* princess, but that just showed him how naïve he could be. It irked him when he thought that she and that mealymouth James Bannings were together, maybe even having a good laugh over all this, over him, the hick rancher who'd been dumb enough to fall for her.

"I can't help you, Drummond," Liam was saying. "In fact, I don't think anyone can help you but yourself."

"Yeah, sorry to have bothered you," Quinn mumbled darkly, retreating.

The sight of the ordinarily easygoing rancher looking so dispirited as he began to walk away caused Liam to have some second thoughts on the matter. He didn't care to be related to those people, true, but his mother had embraced it. Maybe she knew more than he did. She sure couldn't know any less.

"Hey, Drummond."

Quinn stopped walking as Liam called his name.

"Yes?" The single word vibrated with unspoken hope.

"Why don't you go talk to my mother?" Liam suggested. "Chances are she probably doesn't know anything helpful, either," Liam warned the other man, not wanting him to get his hopes up too high. "But then, on the other hand, you never know."

He'd heard one of his brothers saying something about his mother staying in touch with this new sister she had suddenly become aware of. If that was true, then maybe she knew something about this Amelia person, who apparently had Drummond tied up in knots.

Quinn appeared to visibly brighten at the suggestion, flashing a wide, grateful smile. "Thanks, Liam," he called back.

"Yeah, well, good luck to you," he responded, turning away.

As for him and his own problem, Liam thought, he was going to need a lot more than just plain luck. He was going to need a miracle or two—or eight—because that snobbish Julia Tierney gave him the impression that when she latched on to something, it would take a stick of dynamite—if not more—to get her to let go and step back.

It was up to him, he thought, to find that so-called

dynamite stick so he could separate her from this "cause" she had taken up and get her to clear away the cobwebs from her eyes.

None so blind as those who refuse to see, he couldn't help thinking. He just needed to find a way to make her see.

Good luck to me with that, he thought as he got into his truck. He'd see what could be done tomorrow, he promised himself. As for now, what he needed was a good night's sleep, something that had been eluding him of late. He hoped he'd finally get it tonight.

Although he really had his doubts about that.

Chapter Six

The idea came to Liam the following morning.

He wasn't exactly sure when or how it had actually occurred to him, but out of the blue, the adage about a picture being worth a thousand words seemed to burst on his brain as he was having his first cup of eye-opening coffee before heading out to begin his morning chores on the ranch.

In this case, the so-called "picture" that rather nicely took the place of long-winded rhetoric was a restaurant in Vicker's Corners, a town that was located some twenty miles from Horseback Hollow.

Liam had had occasion to drive over to Vicker's Corners a month ago and he remembered thinking to himself as he passed it that the restaurant seemed just too fancy for him—he preferred The Grill. The Grill right here in town. It was more down-to-earth.

But the Vicker's Corners' restaurant seemed like just the kind of pretentious eatery that it looked like Julia was aiming for. The establishment was supposedly a good place for couples looking for a romantic atmosphere. To him that was just downright lazy. You created your own romantic atmosphere. You didn't expect someone else to do it for you. He sure hadn't had any trouble doing that back in high school, when things like that had been a priority for him.

He had become more serious and down-to-earth these days, but that kind of restaurant had to be what Julia had in mind, he thought. And seeing as how Vicker's Corners was a lot more crowded and noisy than his own Horseback Hollow was, Liam thought if she saw it, it might just prove his point to Julia: that building something like that was going to spoil life as everyone in Horseback knew it.

Making up his mind about the matter, Liam hurried through all the immediate chores he needed to do, left instructions with the part-time ranch hand he had working for him to take care of the rest and headed into town. The sooner he could put this fool notion of Julia's to bed, the better he'd feel.

It had become his personal crusade.

Liam felt certain that if Julia took away her support for the new restaurant, the whole project would just fall apart. She was acting as the Mendozas' go-between. He was fairly certain he had enough sway to get a majority of the town to agree with him if Julia wasn't there to gum up the works.

Now all he had to do, he thought, was to convince Julia to come see the place.

"Have you been to Vicker's Corners lately?" Liam asked her the second he came up behind Julia in the Superette.

She had her back to him—and the front door—as she was busy stocking the refrigerated section with the fresh milk that had come in earlier this morning. Liam's question, uttered in his low, baritone voice and coming from behind her had nearly made her drop the bottle she was holding. Regaining her composure, Julia turned around to look at him.

"And good morning to you, too, Liam," she said, forcing an obviously strained smile to her lips.

"Yeah, good morning," he muttered, brushing the greeting aside. "Well, have you?" he asked again, impatience marking his every syllable.

"Have I what?" she asked, not really sure what he was asking her.

Liam sighed. "You know, for the manager of a place like this, you sure don't act like you pay attention to people when they talk to you."

"People, yes," she corrected him. "You, not so much. Now, either say what you came to say outright or just go about your business, whatever that is, because I'm busy right now." She gestured around the store for emphasis. She had a lot of shelves to restock.

Liam could almost *feel* his temper rising. He was

pretty much of an easygoing guy but there was something about this woman that had him seeing red almost instantly.

For that matter, there always had been, he admitted to himself silently. But that wasn't something that he cared to advertise. It might give Julia the wrong idea about the kind of power she had over him.

"I asked you if you had been to Vicker's Corners lately."

"No," Julia told him. "No need to, really," she explained, reaching for another bottle of milk from the delivery crate her regular supplier had brought in for her.

She'd seen the restaurant that Wendy and her husband owned and ran. That had stolen her heart and she wanted to be in charge of the kitchen at a place just like that so that maybe someday she'd be able to own her own restaurant.

"So you *haven't* checked out that restaurant they've got there," Liam concluded.

Liam had piqued her interest. Why was he pushing this place on her, asking all these questions? "No, I haven't. Have you?"

"I've seen what it's done and is doing to the town," Liam said pointedly.

Julia noticed that he hadn't actually answered her question directly. From his tone, Julia had a feeling that any second now, the former big man on the high school campus was going to start going on and on about the evils of having anything in town but a down-to-earth, bare-bones eatery whose idea of a "selection" was having two things to choose from on the menu.

Instead he surprised her.

"Why don't I drive you down there so you can see what having a place like that in town is like firsthand?" He came around the side of the counter and took out the last two bottles of milk for her, putting them into the display refrigerator.

Julia looked around. There was the usual number of people in the store, so it wasn't particularly busy. But she did have shelves to restock. Her mother had seemed somewhat preoccupied this morning so she didn't want to ask her. That would only leave the part-time clerk who was helping out this morning if she took off.

Julia made up her mind. She was needed here, not running off to a neighboring town with Liam. "I'm afraid that I can't get away," she began.

"Sure you can," her mother insisted, coming up behind her. "Elliot and I can handle the customers," she assured her daughter, nodding toward the clerk. "It's not like we're having a run on the place. Go, take some time off. Enjoy yourselves," she encouraged. "Shoo," she added for good measure, gesturing both of them toward the door.

You'd think her mother would know better than to all but throw her into Liam's arms. "This is a scouting trip, Mother, not a getaway," Julia told her mother in all seriousness.

Annie patted her daughter's cheek. "Then *think* of it as a getaway, dear," she encouraged before looking pointedly at Liam. "See what you can do to loosen her up a little, Liam. She is just much too serious for a girl her age."

He smiled at the older woman, his expression softening his features and making him look every bit as roguishly attractive as he had looked in high school, when he was every girl's idea of the classic exciting bad boy.

"I'll do my best, ma'am," he promised.

Annie returned his wide smile. "That's all I can ask."

"I think I should warn you that I carry Mace in my purse," Julia told him as she walked by, lowering her voice so that only he could hear.

"Duly noted," he murmured without changing his expression or letting it betray him.

As Julia went to the back office to get her purse and shrug out of the oversize apron she always wore in the store, Liam turned toward her mother and said, "Don't worry, I'll have Julia back in the Superette in a couple of hours."

"That hardly seems like enough time, dear," Annie replied, shaking her head and obviously shooting down his initial agenda. "There's no rush to get back— really," Julia's mother insisted. "Julia doesn't take nearly enough time for herself. She's the most selfless girl I have ever known," Annie lamented. The older woman moved closer to him, straining to look up since Liam was a foot taller than she was. "Force her to have fun if you have to. Take the long way home. Enjoy the day, the evening," she elaborated, expanding on her initial instruction. "I was serious when I told you to loosen her up a little. Julia's going to be old someday without ever giving herself permission to be young."

"We're just checking out the restaurant there, Mother," Julia reminded her as she came back. Her purse strap was slung over her shoulder. "Not going for a hayride."

Annie heard what she wanted to hear. Her face brightened at the mention of a hayride. "Now, there's an idea," she declared.

"An idea that is going to lie exactly where it is, Mom." Julia brushed a kiss against her mother's cheek. "I'll be back *soon.*" She put emphasis on the last word. "Hold down the fort until then."

"I was holding down the fort before you were born, my girl," her mother reminded her. "I won't have any trouble doing it again. And you, mind what I told you," Annie told her daughter.

Julia knew that her soft-spoken mother was every bit as stubborn as she was in her own way. This wasn't an argument that she was destined to win even if she stood here for the remainder of the day, so she appeared to silently surrender.

Not that she had any intentions of thinking that this excursion was anything except what it was: an exploratory excursion to check out what would eventually become her competition—*if* she ever got that restaurant built in Horseback.

Julia was aware that she was counting her chickens before the hen had even laid her eggs, but she was really excited about the prospect of this restaurant and what it would mean for her future, for the town's economy.

Julia realized that this was the most alive she'd felt in a long, long time.

Since even before her marriage to Neal.

"Okay, if we're going to go, then let's go," she told Liam.

Liam grinned, waved goodbye to her mother and fell into step beside Julia.

"I thought we'd take my truck, since I suggested the trip. Any objections?" he asked because, knowing Julia, there were *always* objections of some sort to anything he suggested.

"Not yet," she said glibly and then added, "You'll know when I have any."

"I have no doubts about that, Julia," he told her. "I have no doubts at all."

A retort rose to her lips, but she forced herself to swallow it. For now it just might be safer to let things like that just slide off her back. There was nothing to be gained but a headache from any kind of confrontation at the beginning of this trip.

She had no doubt that there'd be plenty of time for that on the way back.

The trip to Vicker's Corners went relatively quickly. The twenty miles between Horseback Hollow and the other town was rather desolate and the only traveling companions they encountered were close to the ground and seemed unfazed by their passage.

It wasn't until he got closer to Vicker's Corners that other trucks as well as a few cars could be seen in the vicinity of the town. Rather than the simple two streets with their quaint, weathered shops that were at the center of Horseback Hollow, Vicker's Corners had stores that he'd heard one of his sisters refer to as "charming." More than a couple of these "charming" stores lined Main Street, attracting a significant amount of vehicular traffic.

And just outside the town proper there was a tall, colorful sign that Liam made a point of calling her attention to.

"See there?" he asked, indicating the sign as if there was any way she could have missed seeing it. "It says they're going to be building condominiums outside of town. Condominiums and 'luxury estates,'" he quoted in disgust, whatever "luxury estates" was supposed to mean. "They're completely wiping out the honest, friendly country life folks around here grew up with, all so that someone can make an almighty dollar profit."

It was going to be an awful lot more than a dollar, she couldn't help thinking. But the idea didn't appall her the way it obviously did him.

"You've got something against earning a living?" she asked, really curious as to what his answer might be.

"I've got something against destroying a living," he countered. "And from what I hear, this all started with that fancy restaurant right there," he told her, gesturing toward the establishment they had come to view.

He made it sound as if the restaurant had some sort of evil powers. She refused to believe that *he* actually believed that.

"They built that place," he went on, "and then everything else you see kind of fell into place around it."

Liam clearly meant it as a criticism. "The shops. The traffic. The 'luxury estates...'" He all but sneered.

Liam obviously thought of it as some sort of pending doom.

She, however, saw what had been achieved as a model for her own goal. But rather than argue with Liam about it, which she knew would happen if she started trying to point out favorable things about the restaurant to him, she decided to try another, more practical approach to the problem in front of her.

"Have you ever been inside the restaurant, Liam?" she asked him.

He stared at her. The question had caught him off guard and he wasn't prepared for it. "Me?"

"Well, I don't see anyone else in the truck and I know I haven't been inside the restaurant. Have you ever eaten there?" she asked, phrasing her question another way.

He debated lying, then decided against it. He had a feeling that somehow she'd know and then she'd dismiss everything he had to say. So he went with the truth, which was a lot simpler to keep track of.

"No, I haven't," he admitted and then asked defensively, "What does that have to do with anything?"

He was kidding, right? The whole point of a restaurant was what was inside it, what it served, the kind of people doing the serving as well as the cooking, not the physical building itself.

"It *has* everything to do with it. Stop the truck. We're going to go in and eat there," she told him with finality, leaving no room for argument.

"Why, Julia Tierney, are you asking me out on a

date?" he asked, pretending to be shocked. He was clearly amused.

Julia felt as if she'd been blindsided.

Had he done this on purpose? Had he deliberately set her up?

Looking at him now, she couldn't decide whether he had, but they both needed to go inside the restaurant and sample the food—he more than she. But she also needed to set Liam straight right from the beginning. Otherwise, she had a feeling she was *never* going to live this down. Not that the idea of going out with him didn't appeal to her, but it would have to have been clear from the beginning—and he would have to have asked her out to begin with, not thrown out a vague suggestion. Otherwise, he would make it out as something she'd done, and there was no way she was going to ask him out on a date.

"No, this isn't a 'date,' this is just research. I wouldn't go out on a date with you," she informed him pointedly. "I wouldn't in high school and I won't now."

When she'd turned him down in high school—the only girl who had—it had stung his ego badly. He was surprised that the memory still bothered him a little.

The difference being that this time around, he knew how to cover things up a whole lot better.

"Don't knock it until you try it," he told her glibly. "There're a lot of women around in Horseback Hollow who can tell you that you're really missing out on something."

"What I'd be missing is my brain if I thought of

this as anything but what it is—research," she stressed with feeling.

The next moment, since he had stopped the truck as she'd asked, Julia got out on her side. Closing the door, she looked in at him. "Well, are you coming along? Or are you afraid that I'm right and you don't want to be forced to admit it?"

That did it for him. Liam was out of the truck in a second, locking it behind him.

"The day I'm afraid of anything that you might have to dish out is the day I pack it in and just give up altogether. You, missy, are wrong—on a lot of counts. And I'm going to take extreme pleasure in proving it to you and in hearing you say 'You were right, Liam' when this is all over."

He walked slightly ahead of her to the restaurant's double doors. The establishment's hours were posted to the right of them. Luckily, they had opened for lunch merely a half hour ago.

Which meant that they were free to go in.

He held the door open for her. "Let the adventure begin," he said.

She looked at him as she walked past Liam and went inside.

"My thoughts exactly," she informed him tersely.

Neither one of them had a clue what the other actually meant by that but there was no way either of them was about to admit that.

Chapter Seven

The atmosphere within the upscale restaurant seemed incredibly tranquil and soothing.

The words *soft* and *romantic* were the first two that sprang to mind when Julia looked around. Instrumental love songs drifted through the air, thanks to a better-than-average sound system. The music was just loud enough to be detected, yet quiet enough not to be obtrusive.

This was definitely a place, Julia concluded, designed for lovers and couples who wanted to become lovers.

She and Liam did not belong here, she thought. But to suddenly turn around and walk out of the restaurant at this point would only seem odd and attract unwanted attention. Not to mention some undoubtedly snappy, unwanted comments from Liam.

They were here so they might as well stick it out, Julia decided, scanning the immediate area for a second time. Maybe she'd learn something she could use when she talked to Wendy and Marcos about the design and theme of the restaurant they were looking to build in Horseback Hollow.

"First time here?" a tall, slender blonde asked them with an understanding smile. She was wearing a name tag and looked every inch the hostess as she indicated that they were to follow her into the dining room.

"How can you tell?" Julia asked. Did they look as if they were so out of place to this woman?

"It shows in your faces," the hostess answered. "I promise you'll be repeat customers soon enough." Her words were accompanied by a light laugh.

Even her laughter was soft, blending in delicately with the rest of the ongoing muted sounds in the restaurant.

As she followed behind the hostess and her eyes became accustomed to the dim lighting, Julia saw that the restaurant appeared to be full to capacity. By her calculation, it had only been open since twelve-thirty. Business was apparently *very* good.

"Is it always like this?" Julia asked the young woman walking ahead of them.

The slender blonde turned around. "No, it's usually a lot busier than this," she replied in all seriousness. "Standardly, we have a long waiting line out front. But if you're wondering, your privacy is guaranteed," she promised. "Will this booth be all right?" she asked, stopping at a booth for two.

The booth was part of several set up along the wall, each one cleverly arranged so that it gave the impression of being isolated from the others, even though it wasn't.

"The booth is fine," Julia replied. "But we really don't need to have our privacy guaranteed," she added.

"Speak for yourself. I don't want anyone to know I'm here," Liam said, waiting for Julia to slide into the booth first so that he could finally sit down himself. He had been hungry for more than the past half hour and his stomach was growling, more than a little impatient, waiting to be fed.

"I wouldn't worry if I were you, Jones," Julia told him shortly. "The kind of people you know wouldn't be found in a nice place like this." Her voice was distant, but that was his fault. He'd stung her pride with his dig about not wanting to be caught in a romantic restaurant with her.

"You two have been a couple for a while now, haven't you?" the hostess asked knowingly, handing each of them a menu.

"No," Liam declared, looking at the hostess as if she had a trifle too many birds perched on her antenna.

"Not even for a few seconds," Julia denied with feeling.

"Sorry, my mistake," the woman said, although she didn't sound as if she was really convinced that she had made one. She paused a moment longer to explain the possible misunderstanding. "It's just that the two of you sounded so intense, I just naturally assumed that you had been together a long time."

"We haven't been together at all," Julia told the hostess with feeling. "We just know each other from high school. Slightly," she underscored.

There was an enigmatic smile on the hostess's lips as she nodded and murmured, "I see." The smile crept into her eyes. "Your server will be here in a few minutes," she promised, then lowered her voice just a touch more before saying, "Enjoy your first time."

"She didn't say 'here,'" Julia said, her voice slightly agitated after the woman had retreated to the front of the restaurant.

Liam stared at her. Julia was babbling, he thought. "What?"

"'Here,'" Julia repeated. "That hostess should have said 'Enjoy your first time *here,*' but she left off the last word."

He didn't see what the big deal was. From where he was sitting, Julia was getting herself all worked up over nothing. "Maybe it was implied and she just forgot to say it."

Julia looked in the direction that the hostess had disappeared. She shook her head. "No, I really don't think so."

"Okay," Liam answered gamely—and then his voice dropped seductively. "So maybe she really meant for us to enjoy our first time."

Julia didn't have to ask him what he meant by that. There was what she could only refer to as a wicked smile curving Liam's rather full mouth and that, in turn, could only mean one thing.

Incensed, Julia raised her chin defiantly. "It would take a lot more than soft lighting and soft music to make that happen."

"Well, according to the hype, the soft lighting and soft music in this place are supposed to be the starting point. That's the purpose for all this, am I right?" he asked her pointedly.

How did she manage to get backed into a corner like this? "Much as I hate to say it, yes, you're probably right," she grudgingly admitted.

Liam leveled a look at her. Ordinarily he didn't mind matching wits and exchanging barbs, but somehow, it just didn't seem right in a place like this. Since they were here—and he was hungry—he made up his mind to make the best of the situation. But only if she wasn't going to be waspish.

He gave her a choice. "Look, you want to bicker or do you want to see what the food is like here?"

He was being reasonable, she realized—and worse, she wasn't. Who would have ever thought—?

"Sorry, you're right. We should order and see what's good." After all, that was why, at bottom, she had come here.

"Wow." He looked properly surprised just before he added, "Alert the media. We came to an agreement."

"So how about we strike a temporary truce?" she suggested.

"Absolutely," he told her with enthusiasm, putting out his hand across the table.

Julia hesitated for a moment, then slipping her hand into his, she shook it.

Their waiter, a tall young man with sandy-brown hair, perfect, chiseled features, gleaming white teeth and no hips to speak of, approached, greeted them un-obtrusively and left them with a basket of warm, crisp bread, pats of butter wrapped in silver foil and the promise to return for their orders "soon."

"At least he didn't recite the specials of the day," Julia commented. That tradition, meant to be helpful, had for some reason always gotten on her nerves.

"Maybe they're all special," Liam quipped. He skimmed the two pages that made up the menu. The specials were listed at the top of the first page. "Or maybe he just assumes we know how to read."

Julia laughed at his comment. Liam could be amusing when he wanted to be, she grudgingly—and silently—admitted.

"What looks good to you?" she asked Liam, glancing over the two long, descriptive columns that comprised the restaurant's afternoon menu.

When Liam didn't answer, she raised her eyes from her menu and began to ask her question again, but the sentence remained stuck on her tongue, unable to move, to materialize. He was looking at her pointedly, answering her question without saying a word.

And just like that, she could feel the room around her growing warmer. Could feel heat creeping up the sides of her neck, threatening to turn everything in its path a unique shade of pink.

Julia's innocent question had instantly brought a single word to his mind as well as to his tongue.

You.

Mercifully, Liam managed to stop the word before it actually emerged and wound up embarrassing both of them. He was rather certain that he wouldn't have had a clue how to talk himself out of that one.

But the incriminating word hadn't been said aloud, so, for now he was safe and as long as he made no slips, everything was going to be all right.

After a beat Liam replied, "Not sure yet. There's a lot of flowery rhetoric to wade through. In my experience, good food speaks for itself. If it can't, it might mean it's not so good after all and it's just trying to pull the wool over your eyes with a lot of pretty ten-dollar adjectives." He decided to give her an example of the point he was making.

"I once bought a watch that was supposed to be waterproof. The ad claimed it 'laughed' at water. One day I accidentally spilled some water on it and not only didn't the watch 'laugh' at the water, it didn't even so much as chuckle. The damn thing died less than five minutes later, never to 'tick' again. The bottom line is if something's good, it doesn't have to convince you of the fact."

"You might have a point," she heard herself saying grudgingly. Maybe all the adjectives that went along with this place were overkill. She made a mental note to herself to be careful of overkill.

"Wow, you agreed with me twice in one day." He pretended to cover his heart to keep it from leaping out of his chest—or worse. "I'm going to get a swelled head."

"'Going to?'" she echoed, dryly questioning his last comment.

"And she's back." Liam couldn't resist mimicking the voice of a radio announcer making an introduction.

"I never left," she informed him dryly.

The waiter returned, looking from one to the other, a silent question in his soulful brown eyes. Julia ordered something referred to as Heaven's Promise, while Liam pointed to an item called Love At Last. The waiter pronounced them both excellent choices and promised to return within a few minutes with their meals.

"You know what you ordered?" Liam asked her after the waiter had left.

"Chicken—" The note of confidence left her voice after a beat. "I think, but I'm not sure."

Liam laughed, nodding his head. "Actually, I think we both did."

"Should be interesting," she ventured, looking forward to comparing the meals once they arrived.

"We'll see," he replied.

He noticed that she was scanning the area again, doing her best to take in the other booths. But they were, as the hostess had promised, arranged so as to maximize the occupants' privacy. He could either watch her, or make small talk. But he had no patience with either.

Instead he decided to ask out of the blue, "So what happened between you and the perfect husband?"

Her head whipped around. Julia looked at him, completely stunned. "What?"

"You and Neal," he elaborated. "Neal seemed like perfect husband material. He was a lawyer, faithful— He was faithful, right?" he asked, checking.

"Yes, he was faithful," she snapped. There was no way she wanted to chance Liam starting a rumor that Neal had fooled around. Neal was one of the good guys and deserved better. She wasn't about to see his reputation dragged through the mud just because Liam happened to have a fanciful mind.

"And he was good-looking—if you liked that all-American look," Liam qualified, making it sound like a minus instead of a plus. "On paper, you two sound perfect for each other. So what went wrong?"

She couldn't believe the nerve of this man. "And what makes you think that's any business of yours?" She really wanted to know.

"Well, we have to talk about something and talking about the weather gets boring fast. But we argue about everything else, so I thought this might be the one topic that was safe to talk about. If you don't want to," he continued gamely, "we could just stare at one another until the waiter comes back. Then we can pretend to be busy stuffing our faces, making it impossible to chew and talk at the same time—"

Julia sighed. He had a point, she admitted grudgingly. And she really didn't mind talking about Neal. She supposed this came under the heading of making the best of an uncomfortable situation.

"Nothing 'happened,'" she finally told Liam. "The marriage had just run out of steam."

That presupposed that there had been steam once

upon a time. He found that a little hard to believe. Neal Baxter had as much vibrancy about him as a prescription tranquilizer.

"Then there was steam to begin with?" Liam asked her.

Ordinarily she would have indignantly replied that of course there had been steam. Lots of it. But the way Liam was looking at her—as if he could read her thoughts—she had a feeling that he knew that "steam" between Neal and her had never been part of the equation. Moreover, that he somehow knew that hers had been just a marriage not of convenience, but a convenient marriage.

"Neal was a really nice guy and we were friends," she told him. "I think we both got married hoping that what we had would grow. Instead, it just stagnated. We were far better friends than lovers." The second the words were out of her mouth, Julia was suddenly stunned that she had actually said that. Flustered, she attempted to cover it up. "What I mean—"

He could almost read her mind and feel her sudden panic—as well as know the reason for it. It wasn't hard to guess.

"Don't worry, I'm not going to quote you anywhere. It goes no further." He looked at her knowingly. "So what you're saying is that there was no spark between the two of you, no flash and fire." It wasn't a guess on his part but a reaffirmation.

"What I'm saying," she told him with conviction, "is that Neal deserves to be happy and I hope he is. Someone told me that he'd gotten engaged recently. If it's true, I just hope the woman realizes that Neal is a very special man and that she's very lucky. I wish Neal and his future wife nothing but the very best."

Liam looked somewhat surprised by her good wishes for a man who had once shared her bed. And she meant that, he could tell by the look in her eyes. It was all too calm and genteel for him.

"You do?"

"Yes. Why?" Why did he look so surprised to hear her say that?

Liam shrugged. "Nothing. You just seem very complacent about all this and that wasn't what I'd heard through the grapevine," he told her.

The grapevine. Not exactly the most straightforward source of honest news, she thought. She didn't bother asking him what it was that he *had* heard. Lies didn't bear repeating, not even once.

"Well, people like to talk, it helps while away the time, I guess. And if the facts make something dull, well, can't have that, can we?" she asked sarcastically. She didn't care for gossip and it was all the worse when it was about her. "But if you want the truth, I really do wish him well."

"Well, my hat's off to you," Liam told her in all honesty. "And him, I guess."

She'd followed him up to a point, but now he'd veered off again. "What do you mean?"

"Well, I take it that you broke it off with him."

She did her best to keep a poker face. "Why would you say that?"

She actually had to ask him that? He found it amusing, but he played along, giving her a reason. "You never struck me as someone who just went along with things if she didn't like the way those things were going." She was nothing if not a scrapper. Maybe that was one of the things that he found attractive about her.

"Well, if you must know, yes, I broke it off with Neal, which is why I'm glad he found someone else." She didn't like having him on her conscience. She could still remember his expression—shock mingled with sorrow—when she'd finally gotten through to him.

"And he went quietly, huh?" Liam mused, seemingly marveled and clearly surprised by the man's behavior.

"Yes. Why?" It was her turn to push the question.

"Nothing." He shrugged carelessly again. "But if it was me and my woman had decided that it was over between us and told me she was taking off, well, I wouldn't just meekly lie there and take it. I'd do something about it. I'd do something about getting her back," he said with conviction. "And I'd do it fast, before she had time to get used to the situation."

"Oh, you mean like hog-tie her and leave her in the barn until she was going to come to her senses?" she scoffed, her voice a mixture between being flip and a tad contemptuous.

"Well, maybe not that—" he conceded, then tagged on, "unless it was a last resort." His reply was followed by a wide, amused grin.

She knew he was kidding, but there was something in his eyes, something about the way he was looking at her, that caused a little thrill to tango up her spine and back down again. For just a fraction of a second, she felt that he was talking about the two of them—even though logically, she silently insisted, he really couldn't possibly be. After all, there was nothing between them. They hadn't even gone out.

And yet...

They looked at one another for what seemed like one of the very longest moments on record, interrupted finally by someone clearing his throat. Belatedly, she looked over to see that their waiter had returned with their covered meals on a cart.

"I can come back later if you wish," he offered, ready to wheel the cart with their meals on it away for a little longer.

"No," she replied to the young man. "You came just in time."

She thought she heard Liam murmur, "Amen to that," but she wasn't sure it wasn't just her imagination giving voice to her own thoughts.

Chapter Eight

"So, what do you think?" Julia asked him as they walked out of the restaurant more than an hour later.

She did her best not to sound eager, not to sound as if his answer was as important to her as it was. They'd talked all through the meal, but he hadn't commented at all about the restaurant, even though she had given him ample opportunity to do so. And, after all, the only reason they were here was to check out the restaurant to see what it had to offer.

Liam was, she thought, a rather difficult nut to crack. During the course of the meal, he had managed to ask her a great many questions about herself while volunteering next to nothing about himself.

Then, again, she probably knew about as much about

him as there was to know. He'd been rather transparent in his dealings in high school.

Still, after the lunch they had just had, accompanied by his twenty questions, he owed her, she decided.

Liam was squinting, trying to acclimate himself to what seemed like intense sunlight at this point after having been inside the dim restaurant for so long. It was a little like emerging out of a cave after a very long, dark winter. "What I think is that it's too damn dark in that place."

She should have known he'd say something flippant like that. The man had a knack for dodging direct statements whenever it suited him.

"Besides that," she countered as they circled to the lot behind the restaurant, where he'd parked his truck. "What did you think of the food, the service, the selection on the menu?" she prompted since the man wasn't volunteering *anything* on his own. After all, that *was* supposed to be the reason they had come to Vicker's Corners in the first place.

Liam shrugged. "They were okay."

"Try not to burst a blood vessel in your enthusiasm," she said sarcastically.

He stopped walking, annoyed with her flippant remark and with the fact that she was trying to get him to agree with her. He'd thought that once she saw how the simple life seemed to be dying back in this town, she'd be willing to admit that he was right in voting against the new restaurant coming to Horseback.

The part that bothered him the most was that he

could see how a restaurant like the one they'd just left might appeal to some people back home.

Irritated, he demanded testily, "What is it you want me to say?"

If she told him what to say, it wouldn't count or carry any weight. "I can't put words in your mouth," she retorted, frustrated.

"Well, you sure don't like the ones that are coming out," he pointed out in frustration. "Look, the place was okay, but so's The Grill. The Grill doesn't try to put on airs. You want to know my requirements for a good restaurant?" It was a rhetorical question on his part because he didn't wait for her reply. He just went on to answer his own question. "Here're my requirements. I like my food to taste good, to be hot and to arrive in something under half an hour. The rest are just added frills. I don't need frills," he said flatly. He saw disappointment flash in her eyes. "Not what you wanted to hear, was it?" He realized that he took no particular pleasure in that.

That should have been his first warning sign.

No matter what, Julia had always tried to find at least one positive thing in any situation. It took some doing this time, but she did find one positive thing.

"I wanted you to be honest and you were honest." They resumed walking again. "Obviously," she continued philosophically, "you're not the target audience the people who own and run that restaurant were trying to reach." She looked around at both the number of vehicles in the parking lot and the people who were passing them, heading for the restaurant's front entrance. "Lucky for them, your reaction isn't typical."

"Never thought of myself as part of the herd," Liam told her, reaching his truck.

"That's good because you're not," she assured him with a small laugh. Julia waited for him to unlock his truck, then got in on her side.

"If you wanted a 'typical' reaction, as you call it, you should have brought your ex-husband here, not me," he told her with a trace of annoyance in his voice. From what he knew about the man, Neal Baxter was the poster boy for the word *typical*.

Glancing to see if she was strapped in, Liam started up the truck.

"Neal moved away, remember?" she said, raising her voice slightly as the engine rumbled to life. "He's not here and you are. Your opinion was the one I decided counted."

He laughed shortly as he drove away from the lot. "You mean mine is the opinion you want to change."

"That, too," she admitted. She gestured toward the sidewalk as they stopped at a light. "Look at all this foot traffic going on."

"I'm looking, all right." And he didn't like what he saw. There seemed to be too many people, in his opinion. Did they all live around Vicker's Corners, or were they just passing by, the way he and Julia were?

She could hear the hostility in Liam's voice and glossed right over it. She knew if she commented on it, she'd be sidetracked into an argument and that wasn't going to lead anywhere except to have her going around in an endless, frustrating circle.

Been there, done that.

"Having the restaurant here is good for everyone's business, not just the restaurant's," she pointed out adamantly.

He saw it differently. "If the people are here, in town, it means they're not working their ranches."

"Not everyone has a ranch," she reminded him.

Yeah, and there was a reason for that, he thought cryptically. "That's because they spent all that time, sitting in a dark restaurant," he told her.

Liam sped up to make the light—the last traffic light before he drove out of town. A minute later Vicker's Corners was behind him and he could feel a sense of relief washing over him.

Most likely just his imagination, he thought—but it still felt good to leave the place.

Julia bit off an inaudible, frustrated sound. "You are absolutely infuriating, do you know that?" she said, struggling not to shout at him.

"The way I see it…" he told her, speeding up just a touch because they were out on an open road, even though it was only two lanes wide. "I'm absolutely right. But have it your way. Which you are," he reminded her. "The preliminary vote went your way. There's no reason to believe that when the final votes are cast, the results will be any different. That means the town's going to let those people come in and build their damn restaurant anywhere you tell them to. Frankly," he said, sparing her a look, "what I don't get is why you're still trying to convince me that building that restaurant is the right thing to do."

She blew out a frustrated breath. She'd asked herself the same question. But even though the answer wasn't logical, it was important to her that he come around about this. "Because I want you to see the merits of having a business like this in town."

He slanted a quick glance toward her. "And if I don't, you'll stop building it?"

That wasn't the point she was trying to make. "No, of course not—"

He rested his case. "Like I said, there's no point or need to convince me."

She tried again. "Maybe I'd just like to have you on board with this."

She still hadn't given him an actual logical answer. "Why? You afraid I'm going to do something to sabotage this fancy eatery of yours?"

Was that it? Did she think him capable of doing something drastic?

As the thought sank in, he could feel himself growing insulted.

"No, of course not."

Although, Julia had to admit, albeit silently, the thought had crossed her mind a couple of times. Not that she believed Liam would actually attempt to destroy anything, but he was very capable of working on changing some of the people's minds about siding with progress in this case.

"Well, then, why is it so important to you that I see

your side of this and agree with you?" he repeated, wanting her to make him understand.

She wasn't about to admit that she *cared* what he thought. He'd just take it the wrong way—although she didn't know what other way he *could* take it.

Frustrated, Julia threw up her hands. "Never mind. Maybe I just need my head examined."

"Maybe," he affirmed matter-of-factly.

She had no idea why he'd said that, but she knew it *really* annoyed her. Annoyed her even more that they *weren't* on the same side of this issue. "You know, I could be gloating that the preliminary vote went my way and I'm not. Maybe you should chew on that for a while," she told him in mounting frustration.

Liam's profile was to her as he looked straight ahead, but she could see that the corner of his mouth was curving. He was *smiling* to himself, she realized angrily. At her expense?

"What?" she demanded.

"Nothing," he answered in a tone that told her that there indeed was something. And that something was a thought that her words had unearthed. Rather than the food for thought she'd believed she'd just given him, what he would rather "chew on," he realized, was her— starting from the toes on up.

There was no denying it. The woman definitely aroused him.

She was certainly not the kind of woman he was accustomed to. Julia was not as voluptuous as he liked them and certainly not as accommodating as he'd gotten used to, but there was just *something* about her.

That flash in her eyes, that mouth of hers that never seemed to stop moving... It just all went to stir him, stoke that fire in his belly that created a yearning for her within not just his loins, but more importantly, in his mind, as well.

That was the part that both intrigued him—and scared the hell out of him.

"Doesn't sound like 'nothing,'" she retorted. "What is it?" she persisted.

"Nothing," he repeated. "Just leave it alone." He issued the warning in a low, terse voice.

"Or what?" she challenged. When he didn't answer, she repeated, "Or what?" more loudly this time. If she did know what was good for her, she wasn't focusing on that now.

"You don't want to know," Liam told her, his tone almost growling the words out.

"I wouldn't have asked if I didn't want to know," she snapped. "I don't scare off easily, Jones. I'm not like those little harebrained groupies you used to surround yourself with in high school," she said, referring to the other girls contemptuously. "I don't hang on your every word but I do give you credit for having a mind and I just wanted to open your eyes and have you see what—"

"Damn it," Liam swore in utter frustration as he pulled over to the side of the deserted road. "Don't you ever shut up, woman?" he demanded.

He didn't leave her any room to answer—not that he actually even *wanted* an answer from her—because at the same time that he asked the question, he'd simultaneously pulled her to him as he managed to press the release button on her seat belt. And before Julia could even begin to express her surprise at both his question and his actions, his mouth was covering hers.

The second that it did, it seemed to open a floodgate of emotions within him. They were so powerful that he found he had to struggle to get the upper hand and not have them take charge of him or drag him under before he knew what was going on.

The only thing that he *did* know was that he wanted her.

Wanted her badly.

More than he had *ever* wanted anyone before—possibly more than he had ever wanted everyone *combined.* The dalliances, the interludes, the trysts he'd had before belonged to the boy he had been—his actual age didn't matter. What he was experiencing now belonged to the man he had just become.

He had a man's appetite and a man's desires.

And, heaven help him, they were all centered on Julia.

Liam had caught her completely and utterly off guard. She knew she should be horrified as well as furious. And scared.

Very, very scared.

Not of him, of course, but *herself.* She was scared of the intensity that had been aroused by this sudden contact, this sudden profusion of feelings—his and hers—that had washed over her.

And scared because she wanted to make love with him.

Make love to him here, on the side of the road, out in the open where anyone could unexpectedly drive by and see them.

This wasn't the kind of reaction she expected of herself and yet, at this isolated moment in time, Julia felt powerless to do anything about it, to cut this intense desire short, to call a halt to what was happening.

Instead she was *reveling* in what was happening because she wanted it so much, probably had subconsciously wanted it for a very long time.

She could feel her body heating with incredible longing.

Maybe this was why she and Neal had never really had a chance together, because there was something in her soul that had been waiting for this.

For *him*.

For Liam.

Somehow, though she wouldn't have been able to say how or why if her life depended on it, she had detected this, been waiting for this to find her. And now that it had, all she wanted to do was to wrap herself up in it and melt into it, become one with it.

And with him.

Damn it, what the hell are you thinking? an angry voice in Liam's head demanded. Where were his morals, his scruples? He was overwhelming Julia, taking advantage of her and this just wasn't right no matter *how* much he wanted her. If they *were* going to make love, the first time couldn't be out in the open like this, like two reckless teenagers without any restraint, grabbing any opportunity that came their way.

To mean something, the first time had to at least be civilized.

In order to mean something? that same voice in his head echoed, mystified. What the hell was that supposed to mean? Since when had he wanted lovemaking to *mean* anything but exquisite release? What the hell was going on with him?

Whatever it was, it had to do with her and the sooner he got himself away from her, the better off he'd be—at least until he could untangle all this and think clearly again.

So with what amounted to supreme effort, Liam forced himself to back away.

Taking hold of Julia's shoulders—feeling her shaking beneath his hands—he separated himself from her.

An incredible feeling of desolation and loss swirled through him so quickly, Liam thought he was hallucinating. Self-preservation had him instantly shutting down so that he would stop feeling altogether.

"Sorry," he said gruffly. "I shouldn't have done that. Won't happen again," he added stoically.

Buckling up again, he turned on the ignition. Then, staring straight ahead, he pulled his truck back onto the road and drove toward Horseback Hollow.

"You're 'sorry'?" she echoed, then repeated with both bewilderment and anger, demanding, *"'Sorry'?"*

"That's what I said," he answered in a voice so devoid of any feeling it could have easily belonged to a robot.

Julia sucked in a lungful of air. Liam had all but incinerated her world, stirred up longing and desire to a degree she had never even *dreamed* existed and he was *sorry?*

Just what was that supposed to mean?

And what had that just been? An exercise in mind control? In complete and utter disarmament of her body and soul?

She'd been all ready to make love with him and he—

He'd been what? Experimenting with her? Trifling with her?

"What the hell do you think you're doing?" she demanded just as the town began to come into view.

She realized that Liam had to have been doing ninety to get back as fast as he did. Maybe his goal was to somehow crack the time barrier and get back to Horseback Hollow before they had even left so that what had just happened could be wiped out.

So he didn't have to bear any responsibility for it.

"Making a big mistake, apparently," he told her, his voice just as dead and emotionless as before.

The answer couldn't have hurt any more than if he had stabbed her.

The second they reached the outskirts of town, she unbuckled her seat belt, opened the passenger door and jumped out as she angrily shouted, "I'll walk!" tossing the words over her shoulder.

Liam slammed on his brakes, afraid she'd really hurt herself. He reached to grab her but it was too late.

She was already out.

Landing on her feet, Julia ran home without looking back.

He watched her go, wishing with all his heart that he had never suggested going to see that damn restaurant in Vicker's Corners.

Because he had just opened a door to something that wasn't going to be easily shut again and more than likely, what was contained behind that door was going to lead to his undoing.

Chapter Nine

He'd lost sight of what was important.

He had allowed himself to get sidetracked without realizing it, Liam thought, more than a little annoyed with himself. What was important here was the ultimate fate of the town, not the fact that when he'd pulled off the road that day he and Julia had gone to Vicker's Corners and kissed her, his insides twisted up so badly a corkscrew would have looked completely straight by comparison.

The first couple of days after that, he had deliberately thrown himself into working on the ranch, going from first light to beyond sundown with hardly a letup. He thought if he worked hard enough and long enough, his mind would become blank, having no room for anything more than putting one foot in front of the other and simple, basic instructions.

He should have known better.

Exhausted, he'd fallen onto the first flat surface he came to within his house and slept—not the sleep of the just or even the sleep of the weary, too tired to even think. Instead he'd slept the sleep of the troubled—and dreamed.

Dreamed of a blue-eyed redhead and a desire that set fire to his very insides. And when he woke up, he wasn't rested; he was even more tired than when he'd fallen asleep.

At this rate, he'd burn himself out in a week and nothing would be accomplished. Avoiding all contact with Julia wasn't working. This was obviously not a matter of out of sight, out of mind. The only thing that was going out of his mind was him.

That's when the idea came to him. Rather than trying to deny what he was feeling—because that certainly wasn't working out—he made up his mind to *use* that very same intensity to gain the goal he was shooting for: stopping the restaurant from being built and keeping those Fortunes out of Horseback Hollow before they could get a toehold. And the way he was going to do that was to turn on the charm he'd relegated to the sidelines, pursue the woman who was currently haunting his thoughts and seduce her not just into sharing his bed but his philosophy about Horseback Hollow, as well.

The second he formed his plan, Liam smiled to himself. Smiled for the first time in almost a week.

This was going to work, he promised himself. And

maybe, just maybe, after this was over, after he'd bedded her, he'd be over Julia, as well, and could get back to life as he knew it.

It gave him hope.

Damn it, Julia upbraided herself. What was *wrong* with her?

Why did she keep looking at the door, hope springing up within her chest every time she heard that silly little bell go off, alerting her that another customer had walked in?

She knew why, Julia thought sullenly, because even after six days had gone by—six days without so much as a *single* word—she was *still* hoping to see that big, dumb lout walking into her store. She'd always known that Liam Jones was as shallow as a puddle, so why was her pulse doing these stupid, erratic things every time she thought he was walking into the Superette?

He probably had enough supplies up at that ranch of his to see him through six months without needing to restock—and when he ran out, most likely he'd send one of his brothers to buy supplies for him.

She was supposed to be smarter than this, Julia silently insisted. She'd always prided herself for having more brains than those worshipful groupies that had always clustered around Liam back when they were in high school. Why in heaven's name had she suddenly voluntarily joined their club?

"I haven't," she declared staunchly.

"You haven't what, dear?" her mother asked, turning from the magazine display she was rearranging.

"Um, I haven't a clue what I did with that inventory list from last week," Julia told her mother, silently congratulating herself on her quick thinking. She'd been so preoccupied thinking about that idiot that she hadn't even realized she had said anything out loud just then.

She was going to have to exercise a little more control over herself, she thought.

"It's on your desk in the office. I saw it there earlier." Her mother looked at her, concerned. "Are you sure you're feeling all right?"

Julia waved her mother's concern away, feeling slightly guilty about giving her mother something else to worry about. She'd remained here in Horseback Hollow all these years to *help* her mother, not give her more to worry about.

"I've just got a lot on my mind, Mom, that's all."

Annie shook her head. It was obvious that she was in agreement with her daughter.

"You take too much on yourself, Jules. Why don't we hire more help?" she suggested. They already had five part-time workers here at the store as well as two full-time employees. "We're doing well enough to afford it, honey," Annie pointed out.

Now her obsession with that jerk was going to cost them money? Not if she could help it, Julia silently promised.

"We'll talk about that tonight, Mom. With Dad," Julia added.

Annie smiled at her only child. "You're a good girl, Jules, to include your dad like that. After all the work you've put into keeping the Superette open and running, anyone else would have just shut him out."

"Hey, I want him to get well enough to run this place again with you," Julia told her mother, even though they both knew that was probably never going to happen. But for each other's sake—as well as for Jack's—they pretended that it would.

Annie squeezed her daughter's hand, mutely thanking her. When the bell over the door went off this time, Julia didn't bother turning around.

Not until she heard his voice.

"Good afternoon, Mrs. Tierney. Would you mind if I had a word with Julia alone?" Liam asked politely.

"Absolutely not," Annie told him, letting go of her daughter's hand and stepping back. She smiled warmly at Jeanne Marie's son. "She's all yours, Liam."

"I'd rather be staked out next to an anthill," Julia declared, her eyes shooting daggers at the man who had haunted her dreams *every single night* since she'd gotten back from Vicker's Corners.

He had his damn nerve, she fumed, first reducing her to a palpitating mass of desires and longings, then completely ignoring her for nearly a week only to waltz in here as if nothing had happened between them—as if the world hadn't been reduced to a pinprick when he'd kissed her like that.

"Choose it well," she told him as her mother went to wait on a customer at one of the checkout registers.

"Choose what well?" Liam asked, puzzled.

"The 'word' you want to say to me," Julia said to

refresh his memory, "because I've got a really good one for you—that can't be repeated in polite society."

He just bet she did, he thought, tickled despite himself.

The only way to deal with whatever insults and accusations Julia was going to heap on his head, he thought, was to head her off before she ever had a chance to say any of them.

"And it probably isn't even strong enough," he told her, doing his best to look contrite and remorseful. "I acted like a horse's ass," he readily admitted.

"Not even nearly that good," she returned. Her eyes narrowed to intense, accusing slits. "What are you doing here?"

He dug deep for his sincerest voice. "I came to apologize for the way I behaved—and to tell you that I'd like to start over."

Just what was his angle? she wondered. "Start *what* over?" she asked suspiciously.

"Us. You and me," he told her simply, his eyes meeting hers. He knew if he so much as looked away for a second, it was all over for any chance he had to get to her.

"There is no 'us,'" she informed him tersely. "There's not even a you and me. There's me and there's you. Separate," she pointed out.

"Look, whatever name you want to call me, whatever insult you want to hurl at me, I more than deserve. But I felt something back there that day on the side of the road," he told her in a low voice, taking care that it didn't carry to anyone. "I'd like to give it a chance to take root and grow."

"All the great plagues started that way," she reminded him contemptuously, "taking root and growing."

"This isn't like that," Liam protested.

Her eyes narrowed accusingly. "It's *exactly* like that. I don't know what your game is, Jones, but I'm not playing, so why don't you just pick up your marbles and go home?"

"No game," he told her, holding up his right hand as if he was taking an oath. Glancing to see where her mother was, he saw that Annie was busy. But any second now, the woman would turn around and see them, possibly even decide it was time to join them again. He didn't want to be interrupted until he was finished.

Taking her arm, he pulled Julia over to an alcove for more privacy. "You can't tell me that you didn't feel something back there on the side of the road that day."

She looked at him defiantly, echoing his words back to him. "I didn't feel something back there on the side of the road that day."

His eyes held hers. "I don't believe you."

"That is not my problem," she informed him, "and if you don't let go of me, you're going to find out what a problem really feels like."

Reluctantly, because he didn't want to attract any attention to what was going on, he released her arm. "I just wanted you to know that I've been thinking these past few days—"

"First time for everything," she quipped dismissively.

He ignored the dig and just forged on. "And I think

that you might be right about the restaurant. About it being a good thing for the town."

Surprised, Julia looked at him incredulously. "Nobody told me that hell was freezing over."

He smiled at that. He was making headway one small step at a time. "I thought that maybe we could talk about it some more over dinner."

"At The Grill?" she ventured, thinking that was what he had up his sleeve, to subtly show her how more than adequate that eatery was for the locals.

"No—" Liam started, but he didn't get a chance to tell her what he had in mind.

"You want to go back to Vicker's Corners?" she asked him, surprised.

"No," he said patiently, forging on this time. "I thought that I'd have you up to the ranch— I cook," he told her.

She didn't know whether to laugh out loud at the idea of Liam attempting to actually cook something edible, or to be concerned because he had apparently lost his mind. "You cook," Julia repeated.

"That's what I said," he confirmed, his voice unshakably confident about the ability he had just professed to possess.

"And have people eaten what you've cooked?" she asked. "Are they still alive so I can question them?"

"Every last one of them," he assured her. "I can print up a list of names for you if you'd like," he offered, taking what he assumed was a joke on her part and raising it to the next level.

"I'd like," she told him without so much as cracking a smile.

Well, that told him one thing, he thought—not that it was anything new on her part. But then, he'd known when he'd decided on this course of action that it wasn't going to be easy.

Nothing about Julia Tierney had ever been easy.

He supposed that was part of what he'd found so compelling about her—not that any of that mattered right now.

All that mattered was preserving Horseback Hollow the way it was.

"You don't trust me," Liam said.

The old, polite Julia would have denied it, or tried to explain why she had reservations. The Julia who hadn't gotten a decent night's sleep in a week congratulated him on his insight.

"You're catching on."

"You're going to have to learn to trust me sooner or later," he predicted.

The hell she did, Julia thought. "Why?" she asked flatly. "Why do I have to learn to trust you sooner or later? Why do I have to trust you at all?"

"Because I can be a help with this restaurant thing. You still face having to get that final vote from the town at the mayor's next meeting and you still have to convince those friends of yours—the Mendozas, was it?—that Horseback Hollow is the right location for their new business."

Liam had done a complete about-face in six days. Something didn't feel right to her. "Why this sudden change of heart?" Wanting to know, she pinned him down with her eyes. Dared him to come up with something believable.

He plumbed the depth of his being for sincerity. "Because I realized that I was guilty of putting my own feelings about the Fortune family ahead of the town's welfare."

That sounded a great deal more noble than she thought that Liam could *ever* be.

"I thought you said you believed that having that sort of high-traffic restaurant here was going to be bad for the town's 'welfare,'" she reminded him.

He'd found that it was always best to keep his story and his answers simple. That allowed for fewer mistakes to be made. "I was wrong."

"Just like that?" she asked him skeptically. He was nothing if not stubborn. This just felt way too easy to Julia.

"Sometimes it happens that way," he told her innocently, shrugging his shoulders for emphasis and as a testimony to his own mystification. "Have dinner with me and I'll tell you about my ideas. You might find them helpful." He looked at her pointedly, his eyes all but delving into her very soul. "C'mon, say yes," he coaxed. "What have you got to lose?"

A great deal if I actually bought your story.

She continued to play along, but she was beginning to entertain the idea that whether he was serious about his conversion or not—and she had a hunch it was "not"—she could make him believe she was hanging on his words until she was ready to spring her own trap. A trap that would get him to do what *she* wanted rather than him having convinced her that his opposition to her plans was justified.

"I don't know," she replied honestly. "But I'm afraid I'm going to find out."

He couldn't put his plan into action unless he got her up to his ranch. He decided to take an even bigger risk than he was already undertaking and proposed a compromise.

"If it makes you feel any better, you can bring your mother with you, Julia—or anyone else for that matter. I just want a chance to talk to you away from the store and any distractions."

If it makes you feel any better.

Julia knew how that sounded. It sounded as if she was afraid of him and she wasn't. She'd known Liam Jones most of her life and in his own way, he was as honorable as they came. He never took a woman against her will—he just made her very, very willing.

She supposed that she could have dinner with him and hear him out. If he actually was on the level, she really *could* use him to convince the few diehards on the council who might make pushing this vote through difficult for her.

And if her plan worked, then she would *really* wind up turning Liam and bringing him into her camp.

She made up her mind.

"I don't need to bring anyone with me to act as a chaperone," she informed him.

He pretended to give her every chance to change her mind. "You're sure?" he pressed.

"I'm sure," she said firmly and then asked, "What time do you want me to come over?"

He was leaving nothing to chance. She could always change her mind at the last minute and not show up. "I'll pick you up," he told her.

She wouldn't have been Julia if she made this an easy win. "I know my way. I can drive up."

This was turning into a tug-of-war, but then, he would have expected nothing less of Julia. An easy win was a win he held suspect.

"A gentleman always picks up a lady," he told her simply.

She pretended to be surprised by his statement. "You're bringing a gentleman?"

"Very funny," he quipped. He also knew that if he pushed too hard, Julia would back away quickly. It was like a tango, two steps forward, one step back. "All right, suit yourself. Dinner's at seven."

Julia inclined her head. The first round was hers. "I'll be there," she promised.

And she fervently hoped it wasn't going to wind up being something that she would end up regretting.

It's up to you, a little voice in her head said, *to make sure that it won't be.*

She looked up at Liam and said, "And now, if there's nothing else, Jones, I have got to get back to work—or dinner's going to wind up being something I have to cancel."

He raised his hands in a universal sign that he was backing off. "Already gone," he assured her. "Tonight. Seven" were his parting words.

Chapter Ten

Driving to Liam's ranch that evening, Julia almost turned her car around twice.

She talked herself out of it the first time, but the second time she almost succeeded in talking herself into not going. She would have probably made it home if it wasn't for the fact that she *knew* Liam would say that she'd chickened out. The problem was that he would be right. That one small fact would wind up giving him power to lord it over her.

Power over her that she absolutely refused to allow him to have.

So she squared her shoulders, turned around one last time and headed for his ranch. She had to drive as if the devil himself was behind her to make it on time. She'd never been late for anything in her life and she wasn't about to let this be the first time.

Telling herself that she wasn't making a mistake she would wind up regretting, Julia walked confidently up to Liam's front door—in case he was watching—took in a long breath and knocked.

Liam opened the door before her knuckles had a chance to meet the dark wood twice. "You came."

She couldn't tell if he was more surprised than pleased or the other way around. The expression on his face was a combination of both.

"Didn't you think I would?" she asked him as she walked past him and into the front room of his home.

From what she could see, it was a small, sturdy ranch house, very masculine, very him. She remembered hearing somewhere that Liam and his brothers had built it together. They did good work, she couldn't help thinking in admiration.

"Let's just say I wasn't placing any bets on that one way or another," he told her as he closed the door behind her.

The sound reverberated in her chest but she congratulated herself on her poker face. "Since when did you become so cautious?" she asked, keeping her voice light, amused. "You used to be reckless."

He shrugged, leading the way into his kitchen. Intrigued by the hint of aroma she detected coming from that direction, Julia didn't need to be prodded to follow him.

"I grew up," Liam told her matter-of-factly.

"Oh. When? Sorry." Julia laughed dismissively in the

next breath. The jab she'd just taken at him wasn't really fair. "I just couldn't resist. You don't usually leave yourself that wide open."

Something on the grill in the center of his stove top was sizzling and Liam turned down the heat. "I'll be more careful next time. Are you hungry?"

She'd half expected the kitchen to look like a tornado had passed through it, leaving a fire in its wake. Instead everything appeared relatively neat, with several dishes of varying sizes drying on a rack next to the sink. In addition to the main course on the grill, she noticed that the oven was on. Was he baking something in addition to grilling?

"At the moment, I'm more curious than hungry," she confessed.

He switched off the oven. Whatever he had in there was done. "Curious about what?"

"About what you think passes for 'cooking.' The Superette has a fairly well-stocked frozen food section," she reminded him. Although, she had to admit she'd be hard-pressed to match frozen food to the aroma of what he was making on the grill. The oven was a different matter. Maybe Liam had made one thing himself and whatever was in the oven was his backup in case he messed up what he was cooking on the grill.

Liam looked amused by her implication. "Did you see me buying any frozen food?"

She was keenly aware of every time he came into the store—which definitely was *not* often. However, she was not one to give up easily. "No, but you have brothers and sisters who could do the buying for you," Julia pointed out.

"Were any of *them* in today—or yesterday for that matter?" he asked, glancing at her for a second.

Opening the oven door, Liam grabbed a towel in one hand and used it to extract the potatoes he had baking in the oven. He took them out one at a time and deposited them on the counter.

"No," she answered grudgingly. "But that still doesn't mean that you actually cooked the meal you're going to serve."

He took a chilled bowl from the refrigerator. As he put that on the counter, as well, she realized it was a bowl of salad. Nothing fancy; lettuce, quartered cherry tomatoes, diced-up peppers—green and red—and a host of bacon bits spread out in a layer across the top. She still couldn't picture him chopping and shredding, even though she basically had the evidence right there in front of her.

"If you're so skeptical that I can actually cook, you should have been here earlier so you could have watched me making the meal from scratch." He turned the heat beneath the main course off altogether and turned to look at her. The amused smile on his face widened. "Why is it so important that I'm the one cooking the meal, anyway?" His eyes teased hers.

"No reason. I would have just been impressed, that's all," she answered in a low voice that told him she already was impressed and it was killing her.

"And you don't want to be impressed by me, is that it?" he noted.

Fidgeting inside, Julia still didn't look away. She wouldn't allow herself to do that. When she was a kid, the first one to look away in a staring contest lost. Old habits died hard, she realized.

"I didn't realize that the predinner appetizer was going to be twenty questions," she said.

"Fair enough," Liam allowed, then told her, "Dinner's almost ready." The spareribs he'd been grilling were almost done. They just needed a couple more minutes to reach their full flavor. "Would you like a drink while we wait?"

She would have loved a drink to help calm the sudden flurry of butterflies that had come to life and were now circling around in her stomach, growing to the size of vultures.

But a drink would also loosen her up and loosened up was *not* the state she felt she should be in right now. Not when she was alone with Liam and he was looking far better than a man had a legal right to be.

"A glass of water will be fine," she told him.

Liam frowned. "Water is for swimming in. Don't you want something with taste to it?"

Julia thought for a minute, then told him, "Okay. "Orange juice."

"Orange juice it is," Liam replied, taking the bottle out and reaching for a glass. "You want a shot of anything with that?" He nodded toward the bottles of alcohol clustered in the see-through portion of one of the cabinets.

"Just straight-up juice is fine," she answered.

He filled the glass and then handed it to her. "Is it

that you don't drink alcohol or that you don't trust your-self once you've consumed some alcohol?" he asked.

"I have never not trusted myself," she informed him, "and I drink alcohol on occasion, but this isn't one of those occasions." A look of defiance entered her eyes. "I want a clear head when I'm sampling your culinary endeavors."

Replacing the bottle of juice back into the refriger-ator, Liam shut the door. "Wouldn't have it any other way," he told her glibly.

"So, what are we having?" she asked, wanting the conversation to go into neutral territory.

"Besides a truce?" he asked her, the amusement back in his eyes. "We're having grilled spareribs—" he nod-ded at them, then at the counter "—a salad and baked potatoes. Simple," he proclaimed.

"Sounds good," she told him, although she was still having trouble seeing him as someone who could actu-ally put together a meal that didn't involve removing it from a box and peeling back some plastic wrap.

"So," Julia began, taking a steadying breath, "what can I do?"

Liam looked at her, slightly confused. "What do you want to do?" For once, he hadn't meant it as a leading line—although once the words were out of his mouth, there was a wide, inviting grin punctuating the end of his sentence.

Julia tried again. "Let me rephrase that. What can I do to help with the meal?"

He was going to say "Nothing" since the meal was already done, but he could see she wanted to keep busy.

He could understand that. "Well, I haven't put the plates and other things out yet. You can do that if you want to. Dishes are over there." Liam nodded at the far cabinet. "Knives and forks are in the drawer directly below them. You can put them outside."

"Outside?" Julia questioned.

"Yeah, I thought we'd have dinner on the patio. It's a nice night," he told her needlessly. "Unless you'd rather eat in the kitchen. Choice is yours," he added, thinking she would feel more secure if she made some of the decisions herself. He didn't particularly care where they ate dinner as long as they ate it.

She supposed that having dinner outside might be a pleasant change of pace. "Outside is fine," she told him. Armed with plates and utensils, Julia opened one of the double doors that led outside.

Liam was right, she thought. It *was* a beautiful night. Possibly a tad *too* beautiful, she decided on closer scrutiny. A woman could lose her head, not to mention her heart, on a night like this.

She was just going to have to be on her guard, that was all, Julia warned herself.

But to come back inside and suggest that they stay indoors for dinner would make Liam think she was afraid to be alone with him on a moonlit night. The last thing she wanted was for him to think that. That she was some kind of pushover like the other women he was used to.

She knew she'd damaged his ego that time she'd turned him down for a date—her refusal was the only "black mark" on his so-called dating calendar. Every other girl in high school had all but fallen at his feet—

and a couple had, literally. These days, though, she knew Liam was too busy being a rancher to actively seek out the company of fawning women.

Maybe he *had* grown up, she thought.

Julia came back inside to get napkins and glasses, including hers, which was still more than half filled with orange juice.

As she reentered the kitchen, Liam looked up from what he was doing. "I was going to send out a search party. Thought you'd gotten lost."

She lifted a shoulder in an indifferent shrug. "Didn't know that there was a time limit for setting the table."

"There isn't. I just thought that maybe you had second thoughts about having dinner like this with me and circled out to the front of the house to where you parked your car."

She stared at him, insulted that he thought she was running away. "And what? Hightailed it home? You're not that frightening, Jones."

"Never thought I was," he told her mildly. Still, he was fairly certain it had crossed her mind. "Okay, dinner's ready," he announced as he picked up the serving platter. It was filled to overflowing with spareribs and she had to admit that the aroma was activating all sorts of salivary glands, making her mouth water.

Walking in front of him, Julia opened the door leading to the patio for him, then set down the glasses and napkins she'd brought.

"Looks good," she told him.

"Tastes better," he assured her.

Julia laughed, shaking her head. "Not much on modesty, are you?"

He looked surprised at her comment. "I thought you were the one who valued honesty."

"Touché," Julia replied, inclining her head and giving him the round.

Next he brought out the salad and the baked potatoes, carrying both items on a serving tray that, once emptied, he set on its side next to the door. He was going to need it when he took everything back inside after they'd finished eating.

"Okay—" Liam gestured toward the table "—don't stand on any formalities. Dig in," he urged her.

Despite what he'd just said about not standing on any formalities, Liam surprised her by waiting until she had taken a seat and then helping her move the chair in close to the table.

"All right, now I'm impressed," Julia told him honestly as he circled around to his own chair and sat down. "Cooking and manners—what other things have you got hidden up your sleeve?" she asked.

He gave her a look that was nothing if not the last word in innocence as he said, "Not a thing, Julia. Not a thing."

It was the innocent look that did it. She realized at that moment that she was in big trouble, but her stubbornness, not to mention her pride, kept her seated where she was, refusing to get up and flee.

But when she looked back later, reviewing everything, Julia knew that was exactly what she should have done: fled.

"Well?" Liam had done his best to be patient, but Julia had taken, by his count, five bites of her sparerib when by all rights, it should have taken just one bite for her to find out if she liked it or not.

Julia raised her eyes to his, doing her best to choose her words well, but her wonder and surprise got in her way.

"I'm speechless with amazement," Julia finally admitted. He watched with pleasure as a smile bloomed on her lips.

"So you think it's good," he concluded. It didn't hurt anything to get a real compliment out of her.

"No," Julia corrected, then paused just long enough to bedevil him before she added the kicker. "I think it's *better* than good. Who taught you how to cook?" Surprisingly, she wanted to know.

"Nobody," he replied honestly. "I watched my mother a few times and I guess it kind of stuck. It's a basically simple recipe," he went on to tell her, knowing she'd ask eventually. "I make this sauce, stick it and the spareribs into a plastic bag and let them stay in the refrigerator for twenty-four hours before I grill the ribs. No big deal, really."

"Hold it. Back up," Julia cried, all but holding her hand up like a traffic cop. "You *make* this sauce?"

He'd been cooking ever since he'd been on his own and didn't really see what the big deal was. "Yeah, that's what I said."

"Interesting. I just can't picture you like that," she told him in all honesty. She figured he deserved honesty from her after he'd gone to this sort of trouble, making the dinner. "Making trouble, yes. Making your own sauce, no. Who *are* you?" Julia asked him with a laugh as she leaned back in her chair as if to get a better, more critical view of the man who was seated at the table with her.

"Obviously not the person you thought I was," Liam answered glibly.

"Obviously," she agreed, echoing his intonation. "Do you have any other hidden talents?" she asked again, then instantly realized she'd set herself up by using that wording. "That it would be safe for me to know about?" she added.

He smiled at her over the glass of beer he had poured for himself. "I don't know. What's your definition of safe?" he asked.

The look in his eyes was pulling her in. She could all but literally *feel* the magnetism radiating from him.

Not you, she thought. *You are definitely not safe for me.*

"Not getting into a compromising situation with you," she said out loud.

It was supposed to come out sounding terse and off-putting. Instead it almost sounded like a challenge, a dare issued with secret hopes that the challenge would be met and vanquished.

Hurriedly, she changed the subject. Or tried to. "Everything's very good," she admitted, the words all but sticking to her suddenly exceedingly dry mouth. "But maybe I'd better be getting back home," she told him. "I've got to open the store up early and—"

He didn't wait for her to finish making up the excuse she was giving him. "Julia, are you afraid of me?" he asked quietly.

"No!" In contrast, her voice was sharp and somewhat shrill as she answered sharply.

And it was the truth. She *wasn't* afraid of him.

What she was afraid of, again, was herself.

She didn't trust herself to stand fast and hang on to the principles that had seen her through high school— and stayed with her until she'd caught a glimpse of the new, improved Liam.

The problem was that with that torrid kiss she had also glimpsed what she'd been missing and, God help her, she didn't want to continue missing it anymore even though she knew that giving in was the fastest way to send a guy packing.

Especially a guy like Liam, whose longest relationship on record outside of with his own family was two and a half weeks.

"Good," he was saying to her, "because I wouldn't want you to be afraid of me."

Practicing the craft that was all but second nature to him, Liam took her hand gently in his as he looked into her eyes and promised, "I promise that I'll never do anything you don't want me to do."

Julia could feel everything within her tightening up. *Trying* to rally when she knew in her heart, *knew* that it was all but over as far as holding out went.

The problem with Liam's promise was that while he really wouldn't do anything she didn't want to do, at the same time he, just by his mere existence, by looking at her with his soulful eyes, made her want to do all sorts of things as long as those things were done with only him.

Chapter Eleven

Because she felt as if Liam was challenging her to remain, Julia stayed and finished her dinner.

And since prolonged silence would wind up creating a far too tense and pregnant battleground, Julia kept up a steady stream of chatter, talking about whatever came to mind.

They talked about his family, his siblings in general and his mother more specifically. Julia had always liked his mother and she asked him about Jeanne Marie's reaction to discovering that she not only had family outside of her husband and children, but that she was actually one of triplets—and a Fortune to boot.

Little by little, Julia managed to draw Liam out on the subject.

"I guess that for the first time," he said, nursing his

beer, "my mother felt as if she had roots that went back a ways, that she belonged to a family that had a history. Up until that point, she always wondered why she'd been given up. She didn't really talk about it, until she finally had some answers. Ma's like that," he attested. No one had realized how much knowing meant to her until that point.

"Did finding answers to her questions make her happy?" Julia asked.

He thought about the way his mother's face had lit up when the truth had finally come out. It wasn't even the money, which she'd promptly returned, it was the sense of belonging that had pleased her.

But all that was far too much to go into right now, so all Liam said in reply was, "Pretty much."

It was enough for Julia to work with. "Then why do *you* resent the Fortunes so much? Her brother, James Marshall, didn't have to come looking for her and he certainly didn't have to offer your mother her share of the Fortunes' fortune—no pun intended," she added. "Resenting them doesn't really sound reasonable, does it?"

He shrugged. In his heart, he supposed what she was saying was true, but he didn't want to admit it. "Feelings don't have to be reasonable," he told her. "That's what makes them feelings."

In a very odd, off-kilter way, she supposed Liam was right. When you came right down to it, a lot of feelings *weren't* reasonable. What she was feeling right now for him certainly wasn't reasonable.

What it felt like was that she was walking around

with some kind of a bomb inside her that was going to explode at any moment unless she found some way to defuse it.

And quickly.

If she listened closely, she could almost hear the seconds ticking away—synchronized with the beating of her heart.

"Yes, well, I guess that's something you're going to have to work out," she told him, trying to sound offhanded as she got to her feet. Rising from the table, she took a plate in each hand.

Liam rose to his feet, as well. "What are you doing?"

She thought that was pretty self-evident. "Cleaning up."

He put his hands over hers, trying to get her to set the plates down again. "Leave them. I'll take care of it later."

But Julia turned out to be stronger than she looked. And more stubborn, as well. She pulled her hands away, still holding on to the plates.

"No, you cooked, I'll clean. It's only fair," she insisted.

With that, she made her way back into the house and the kitchen.

Liam was quick to follow in her wake, catching up to her in the kitchen. "I never thought about dinner being a battleground for fair play," he told her.

She stopped by the sink, intending to wash off the plates and put them into the dishwasher.

"Just leave them in the sink, then," he urged. He was

behind her and he leaned over to turn on the faucet to rinse off the plates himself.

His goal was to get her to leave the dishes there until later. He had a feeling she was just going to take off if he let her and he didn't want the evening to end just yet. He found he liked talking to her if they weren't engaged in a game of one-upmanship.

And even if they were.

But Julia chose that moment, as he leaned over her, to turn around so that she could voice a protest over his instructions.

What happened next neither one of them consciously intended at all.

But it happened anyway.

Her body brushed up against his, the contact not leaving enough room for a whisper to slip through. She could feel her body temperature instantly rising and as she tried to speak, a single word—no more than a letter, really—got stuck in her throat.

"I—"

Liam couldn't help himself. He'd promised—no *sworn*—to himself that this wasn't going to happen a third time. He wasn't going to just snatch opportunity out of the air and act on it.

Wasn't going to kiss her even though every bone in his body begged him to.

But he discovered much to his surprise that the strength needed to resist Julia, to bank down the high wave of desire that she evoked within him, refused to materialize just when he needed it most.

So down he went for a third—possibly fatal—time…
and he kissed Julia.

Kissed her as if there was no tomorrow, no yesterday,
no future, no past. Only this moment—and he wanted
to make the very most of it that he could.

The instant that resolve echoed in his brain, Liam
gave himself up to the fire that was all but consum-
ing him. The fire that made him realize that tonight, it
wouldn't end with a flash of common sense that would
in turn cause him to pull away because this was, ultimately, all wrong.

This time it was going to end in an entirely different way—unless Julia protested or actually came out
and asked him to stop. She was her own best advocate
because he *knew* for a fact that he couldn't retreat on
his own anymore.

He wanted her that badly.

But she didn't say anything, didn't ask him to stop.
Didn't indicate in any way that she *wanted* him to stop.

And so, one kiss fed into another and another until
he'd lost count just how many there had been.

More than a little, less than enough.

Somehow they had managed to get from the kitchen
into the living room, a trail of hastily removed clothing
marking their path as they navigated the heady seas of
desires fueled with passions.

The more he kissed Julia, the more, he discovered,
he wanted her.

He could feel his body priming, yearning for her and
the mind-spinning feeling of fulfillment that waited just
beyond the torrid meeting of lips and limbs.

* * *

She couldn't think.

For perhaps the first time in her life, Julia couldn't think straight at all, couldn't put together a few coherent words into a sentence. Single words, all revolving around what has happening at this moment, were all that popped into her head.

And dominating them all was one three-letter word. *YES!*

This had to be, she thought, what jumping out of an aircraft was like, the air all but whisked out of her lungs, the ground coming up at her at an increasingly dizzying speed.

It was exhilarating and completely terrifying at the same time.

Terrifying because she had never felt like this before. Hadn't even *imagined* feeling like this before. The word *more* kept echoing in her head over and over again, coupled with an insatiable craving that seemed to have just taken over her entire being.

Arrows of heat shot through her body as Julia felt Liam press urgent kisses along her neck. Kisses that caused a quickening in her loins to such an extent, she was reaching peaks without even knowing she was climbing toward them.

Grasping Liam's shoulders, she dug her fingernails into his flesh, a cry of wonder and joy bursting from her.

Stunned, shaken, she looked at this tall, rugged rancher she'd known since childhood in abject wonder, almost unable to focus at all.

What was incredibly keen was this craving to have

those wild bursts that echoed throughout her body happen again—and again.

And they did.

She felt like sobbing.

She felt like cheering.

And each time another one of these thrilling explosions happened, Julia found herself being propelled just a little higher than she had gone a moment before.

This was something altogether new for her.

She'd had relations with Neal, perfectly good relations, she'd thought at the time, if a little lackluster. But anything that had happened between her ex-husband and herself paled in comparison to what she was experiencing this moment, here with Liam.

When he pressed her back against the deep cushions of his oversize sofa, she arched so that she could feel the hardness of his body against hers. Just the slightest contact was infinitely arousing to her.

When she heard the slight sound of pleasure escaping between his lips, she was empowered to continue, to go higher, because she sensed that while he was trying to be controlled in his responses, she'd tripped a wire within him that set all those sensations she was experiencing free within him, as well.

A sense of triumph echoed through her.

Further proof that what they were sharing was unraveling him, as well, came when she heard him groan, "What the hell are you doing to me?"

Joy cascaded through her because she had proof that this wasn't just one-sided, that she wasn't the only one in this swirling cauldron of wickedly delicious sensations that had so unexpectedly found her.

Julia wrapped her legs around his lower torso as she raised herself up against Liam, a silent invitation for them to become one, to join together and remain united for as long as they were physically able to do so.

If she was lucky, she thought, eternity would find her this way.

It made no sense and Julia didn't care. All she cared about was this exquisite lovemaking she had unwittingly stumbled across.

No wonder all the girls had flocked to him the way that they had. He was an incredible, natural lover. And tonight, he was hers.

Liam couldn't hold out any longer. Wanting to prolong their foreplay for as long as humanly possible for Julia's enjoyment as well as his own, he found he hadn't the power to resist going to the next level indefinitely.

The need within him to savor that final sensation was growing too great.

Gathering Julia to him, his heart racing enough to render him all but breathless, Liam finally entered her. Claiming what was already his from the very first moment that the world had been created.

She didn't think it could get any better.

She was wrong.

It got better.

Incredibly better.

She could feel herself rushing toward the top of the summit, to the farthest point on the star. And then, it happened, the anticipated explosion came and it was so much more than she had thought it would be.

Julia clung to him with the intensity she could have exerted if they were free-falling. Because, in a way, they were.

Slowly, the world came back into focus.

Reluctantly—that seemed to be such a key word in his life these days—the beat of her heart registered as it slowed to something less than the speed of light.

The magic dimmed a little.

Liam went on holding her, not knowing if she wanted him to, telling himself that if she didn't, she would have wedged her hands against his chest and tried to push them apart. He would have released her then, because she'd wanted him to.

But she gave no such indication, so he went on holding her to him. Went on inhaling the scent of her hair— vanilla mixed with lavender—went on savoring the pulses of heat as they went through his body, each a little smaller in magnitude than the one that had come before.

He stayed like that, holding her, until Julia's breathing returned to normal around the same time that his did.

"Was that dessert, or your closing argument?"

Her words, mingled with her breath, were warm against his chest, but he wasn't sure if he had made them out correctly.

If he had, he still had no idea what she was talking about. "What?"

Julia raised her head and looked at him, the ends of her red hair moving slowly and seductively along his flesh, arousing him all over again.

Arousing him almost as much as having her naked body pressed up against his was doing.

"Was that dessert—because we haven't had any—or your closing argument?" she asked again. Julia smiled when she saw the confusion on his face. "When you invited me to dinner on your ranch, I thought you wanted to corner me so you could make your argument against having that restaurant built here."

That had been his initial intention, but that wasn't something he wanted to admit to now, or even briefly touch upon. Not when she'd succeeded in knocking his entire world off-kilter the way she had.

When he had invited her over for dinner, he'd wanted to seduce her. Instead, somehow, though he wasn't sure just how, Julia had succeeded in seducing *him*.

"That would have been underhanded of me," he said, deftly not admitting or denying anything.

"I know." Her face flushed slightly, making him feel guilty over the lie—and attracted as hell to her all over again. "I'm sorry."

"Don't apologize," Liam told her, guilt getting the better of him. "I—"

Her mouth was so close to his, this time *she* was the one who gave in to impulse and lightly, teasingly brushed her lips against his.

It only made her want more, so there was a second pass in the wake of the first. This time she pressed her lips against his just a little harder.

Julia could feel him responding beneath her. Her eyes were laughing as she grinned wickedly. "I guess this is dessert, then," she murmured.

He was aching for her all over again. He couldn't remember *ever* responding so quickly after having just made love.

Nibbling along her lips he asked, "Would you rather have ice cream?"

Only if I could lick it off your body.

The thought, coming like a lightning bolt out of nowhere, startled her. And made her feel that much hotter.

"Nope," she said out loud, not brave enough yet to give voice to her wanton thoughts.

Liam laughed then, catching her up in his arms and rolling so that in one swift, single movement, their positions were reversed and he was back on top of Julia again.

"Me, neither," he told her.

Her heart began to race again as a fresh wave of anticipation washed over her. All she could think about was doing it again.

And again.

"I guess it's official, then. I've joined the crowd," she told him.

He knew she was thinking of the other women he'd been with, the others who had graced his bed or he theirs. But she wasn't just a warm body for the night—much as he wanted her to be.

She was more.

Much as he *didn't* want her to be.

Framing Julia's face with his hands so that all he

could see was her face without any other distraction—
a face that had its own beauty, both inner and outer—
he told her, "You could never be part of a crowd, Julia."

She liked hearing him say her name. It sent a small
shiver down her spine. She knew that some would view
that as an adolescent reaction, but she didn't care. She
still savored it.

"That's a lovely line. Practice it much?" she breathed,
her eyes teasing his, the rise and fall of her breasts
wreaking havoc on the rest of him as they brushed
rhythmically against his chest.

"No. Because it's not a line," he told her just before
he lowered his mouth to hers.

Because she desperately wanted to believe him, to
believe that for at least this small, isolated moment, on
this night, he meant what he said to her, Julia pretended
that it was true.

Tomorrow she could think about how foolish she
was being, to actually believe that she could be special
to him, a man who had had so many women, most far
more experienced than she would ever be.

But tonight, she told herself, she *was* special to him.

Almost as special as he was to her.

Chapter Twelve

Liam was in deep trouble and he knew it.

He had completely lost his edge, his clear perspective, and it was all Julia's fault. The indignation he'd been carrying around about the Fortunes intruding into his life, silently implying by their very existence—at least in his eyes—that he and his family, his *father*, weren't good enough, weren't important in the scheme of things unless they were Fortunes by birth, by marriage or by association, didn't seem to be nearly as explosive as it had been earlier.

He'd even begun to wonder if maybe he'd allowed unfounded anger to get the better of him, letting it dictate his reaction without any substantial evidence to back up his feelings.

After all, it wasn't as if he had been bullied by one

of the Fortunes, or humiliated by one of them, or any one of a number of embarrassing things that would have made him feel slighted.

He couldn't, in all honesty and with a clear conscience, point to a single incident that could be seen as a trigger that had created all this animosity within him.

He was being far too philosophical about this. What the hell was going on with him?

Had making love with Julia brainwashed him? Or had it somehow managed to clarify things for him?

He didn't know.

All he knew was that he was confused. That the anger he had felt about the Fortunes intruding into his and his family's way of life...well, that was gone.

Or maybe it had just gone into hiding.

He decided that if he talked to his father, listened to his father's take on all this—after all, it *was* his name that was being pushed aside to make room for the Fortune surname—he'd get some of his initial fire back.

Or make his peace with it being gone.

One way or another, talking with his father could very well resolve at least *some* things for him.

Leaving a few immediate instructions with his ranch hands that would sufficiently see them through the morning chores, Liam drove off to see his father.

The sooner he got this resolved, the better.

Tomorrow the town was taking a vote on the future of this restaurant that was so dear to Julia's heart. The townspeople had had a week to think about the matter. Any last-minute arguments, pro and con, were going to be made then. He knew he didn't have all that much time to make up his mind whether or not this was a fight he still wanted to have.

After the vote, the restaurant would be a reality or it wouldn't, depending on the outcome.

And the outcome, no matter what it turned out to be, was going to affect him more than he'd dreamed, because this issue had become very personal to him in ways he hadn't foreseen.

Deke Jones looked up when he heard his son's truck approaching.

Used to be, the man thought, that it was the sound of hoofbeats that would draw his attention. But he hardly heard those anymore, other than from the stock he was raising.

For the most part, the sound of hoofbeats only echoed when he was working with his horses, reminiscing about days gone by, or going places that a four-wheel drive vehicle couldn't go.

The tall, lean rancher was a basic, simple man who was satisfied with little, even though he'd always wanted his children to have more—but not *much* more, because that would make them soft and to survive in this world, a person had to be tough. The land was bountiful, but it was also harsh and only the tough managed to make it in Horseback Hollow.

When his second-born came driving up, Deke was busy cleaning the right rear hoof of his favorite horse, a palomino named Golden Lightning.

He'd broken in the horse himself. Broken the stallion in so that Lightning would accept him as his master, but Deke had taken great care not to break the horse's spirit. If he had done that, to his way of thinking it would have been a crime.

"What are you doing out here in the middle of the week, boy?" Deke asked after Liam had gotten out of his weathered vehicle. "Your ma call and ask you to come by?"

"No, I wanted to talk to you," Liam told his father. He leaned against the corral, watching his father patiently scrape away.

Deke went on working, removing debris that had gotten embedded around the horse's shoe. He'd noticed Lightning favoring that leg this morning. To his relief, Deke discovered that the problem was easily rectified. He'd been worried there for a bit that the problem might have been serious. Finding out otherwise put him in a basically good mood—although with Deke, as his wife readily pointed out, it was hard to tell his moods apart.

For the most part, Deke Jones kept everything to himself.

"So talk," he said without glancing up.

Now that he was here, Liam realized that he hadn't planned how he was going to phrase this. After he hesitated for a minute, he admitted, "This isn't easy to put into words."

"I suspect you'll find them if this means enough to you." Deke glanced up just for a second. "I'm not going anywhere."

He and his father had what Liam thought of as an "unspoken" relationship. They didn't talk all that much, but things were just understood. He'd never heard his father talk any more than was absolutely necessary to get his thoughts across—and only as a last resort.

But he needed to have this clarified for him, needed to know if he'd just assumed things and gone off half-cocked when he shouldn't have.

Or if his take on his father's reaction to having the Fortunes suddenly part of their lives was dead-on.

The only way to ask was to ask, right? he told himself just before forging ahead.

"How do you feel about Ma finding out that she's part of the Fortune family and her deciding to take their name and all?" Liam asked.

He knew he was stumbling through this, but it was the thought, not the poetry of the sentence, he was trying to get across. He was fairly confident that his father would know what he meant.

Deke went on working on the hoof and for a moment, Liam thought that his father either hadn't heard him or had decided to ignore the question.

Since it was important to him, Liam tried again. "Dad, how do you feel—?"

"I heard you the first time," Deke answered. Finished, he released the hoof he'd held nestled between his strong thighs while he'd worked.

Golden Lightning whinnied, tossed his mane and haughtily retreated to the other end of the corral, as if to say that he'd been patient long enough.

Brushing off his hands, Deke climbed over the slats of the corral fence and joined his son on the other side.

"How do I feel?" he repeated. "How do you think I

feel after years of breaking my back to put a roof over your heads and food in your bellies?"

It was a rhetorical question so Liam made no attempt to answer him. He waited for his father to continue. The wait wasn't long.

"I was mad, that's how I felt, thinking that maybe your ma didn't think I was good enough and that was why she took on that other name."

His sharp blue eyes narrowed for a moment, pinning Liam in place before he said another word. "Having Christopher take off like that, going to Red Rock to work for those people didn't help matters any." He had his own question and he put it to Liam now. "Did any of you kids feel like you were missing out on anything when you were growing up?"

Deke Jones hadn't been the warmest of fathers when they were kids, but Liam recalled that he had always felt safe, as if his home was his haven and his father was the sentry guarding the gate. Nothing could ever hurt him as long as his father was there. He knew the others had felt the same way.

"We had a great childhood, Dad."

The answer satisfied Deke. He wasn't the kind to milk it for more.

The wiry shoulders rose and fell in a careless shrug. "After I got over being mad, I started seeing things from your ma's point of view. She grew up thinking she was all alone, that whoever her mama was, she just gave her away like yesterday's hand-me-downs. It was nice for your ma to find out that she's got family that wants her.

Not everyone gets that." He let the words sink in and then leveled a look at his son. "Why are you asking?"

Liam was honest in his answer. His father would stand for nothing less. "I just wanted to know if you felt insulted."

Deke shrugged again. "It is what it is. I hear that the Fortunes are good people. That they don't just take without giving back and they don't act holier-than-thou, so unless I'm shown otherwise, that makes them all right in my book." Deke cocked his Stetson back on his head as he looked intently at his son. "We done here?" he queried. "Because I got work to do."

Liam grinned. This had to be the longest conversation he'd ever had with his father. "We're done," he answered. "I've got to be getting back, too."

Deke nodded. "I'll tell your ma you said hi," he said as he walked away.

"Well, you certainly have a spring in your step these past couple of days," Annie noted as she crossed the floor to reach her daughter. They spent a great deal more time together than the average mother and daughter did and Annie was keenly attuned to any changes in her daughter's behavior. "Anything that I should know about?" she asked, a warm, very amused smile curving her lips.

There was no way she was going to say anything about seeing Liam to her mother. Some things were best kept secret, Julia thought. Liam's reputation as a lady-killer had always been larger than life and things like that took a long time to die. She didn't want her mother worrying about her.

It was enough that she knew this was just an interlude and that it would be over soon enough. She was determined to enjoy it while it lasted.

Liam Jones wasn't the kind to settle down with one woman and as long as she didn't lose sight of that, didn't delude herself into thinking that she was unique enough to get him to change his ways, she'd be all right.

But her mother needed a reason for this upbeat swing in her personality, so Julia gave her one. That it also happened to be true was an added bonus.

"I'm just looking forward to the restaurant opening here in Horseback Hollow, Mom. I've been in touch with Wendy and Marcos Mendoza—they're the ones who are looking to expand—told them a couple of the ideas I had for the restaurant, and they really seemed to like what I had to say. I think they might offer me a job once the restaurant is up and running," she said with enthusiasm.

"A job? Why wouldn't they hire you to be the head chef, or the manager, for that matter?" Annie asked. "Why, if it wasn't for you, the council wouldn't even be thinking about this. And you're bright, enthusiastic—"

"One step at a time, Mom. I need some restaurant experience under my belt first." Marcos's explanation about that had made perfect sense to her. No one began at the top. "I *really* want this, Mom. I've always dreamed about being a chef and eventually having my own restaurant, and all this is going to be happening right here," she said, barely containing her joy. "I won't have to leave you or Dad," she added, pleased at the way things had turned out.

Annie had always been very supportive of Julia's dreams, but she didn't want her daughter getting all caught up in a dream before it was nailed down. "Has the final vote gone through?" she asked.

"No, not yet," Julia admitted, but that wasn't going to throw cold water on her plans. This was going to work, she just *knew* it. "But I've been talking to everyone who comes in and I think I've got them all convinced that having a restaurant, a real restaurant, not just a bar and grill, in Horseback Hollow could only benefit the town."

Annie squeezed her daughter's hand. "Don't go getting your heart set on that, honey. Maybe they were just being polite and didn't want to hurt your feelings."

She knew her mother meant well, but what she was suggesting wasn't the case here.

"Mom, I've known these people all my life. They love to argue. If they didn't agree with me, they'd definitely let me know it. No, I think this restaurant proposition is pretty much a sure thing."

Annie still held back. "What about Liam Jones?"

Why was her mother bringing Liam up? Did she suspect that she and Liam had something going on? That when she'd left the store those times, saying she was going back to Vicker's Corners to do further research into the way the restaurant was being operated, she was really going to Liam's ranch?

To Liam's arms?

"What about him?" Julia asked, trying her best to sound as if she was just being mildly curious why her mother would have brought his name up. Trying to act as if her heart hadn't just started beating rapidly at double time.

"Well, I heard him talking here to you that day. He really sounded as if he was dead set against having that restaurant built here and he might just find a way to keep that from happening. I just don't want to see you get hurt, honey."

"Liam Jones can't do anything single-handedly, Mom, and if the town votes to have it constructed—which I know they will—there's nothing much that he can do about it," Julia added.

Annie inclined her head. It *sounded* good. "Still, tomorrow, when the town votes on this at the meeting, I intend to be there. Another vote in favor can't hurt, right?"

Julia laughed. "Right, Mama," she agreed, resorting to the term of endearment she hardly ever used anymore. But this was a special time.

Bending over, she kissed her mother's cheek. "Another vote is always welcome. You realize that when this comes through, we're going to have to hire extra help for you here in the store. But then, I'll be bringing in more money, so we can easily pay for it."

"Whoa," Annie cautioned. "One step at a time. Get this voted in, then you can start thinking about hiring people. And don't worry about the Superette. It'll be hard, but we'll get along without you. We've taken up more than enough of your life as it is. Time you started carving out a life of your own."

The bell over the door announced the entrance of

another customer. Annie automatically looked toward the entrance.

"Right after you wait on this handsome gentleman," she told her daughter, smiling at Liam. "Hello, Liam, how are your parents these days?"

"They're fine, Mrs. Tierney," he replied politely. "Mind if I have a word with Julia?"

"Have as many words as you like, Liam. And while you're at it, why don't you take her off my hands for the rest of the afternoon?" Annie suggested impulsively, much to Julia's obvious surprise. "She hardly ever goes out of the store and she needs to get a little more color in her face."

Liam slanted a glance toward Annie's daughter. A rosy hue was inching its way up Julia's neck and onto her cheeks.

He wondered if Mrs. Tierney suspected that Julia and he were involved. He'd always regarded Julia's mother as a very sharp lady, despite her laid-back, unassuming manner.

For that matter, Liam couldn't help wondering if Julia suspected just how much she had managed to get to him in what seemed to be such an incredibly short amount of time.

"Well, I think she's getting some color in her cheeks right now, Mrs. Tierney," he pointed out, amused by the fact that Julia was actually blushing. "But I'd be happy to take her out for you right now."

"I'm right here, people," Julia said, speaking up as she raised her hand and waved it in front of her mother and Liam. "I can hear you, you know."

"Nice to know that there's nothing wrong with your hearing, dear," Annie said serenely. "Now go," she urged, all but shooing her daughter and Liam out the door. "Have an afternoon outside the store, outside of everything—like a young woman who's not perpetually trying to juggle too many things all at once."

Taking his cue from the older woman, Liam surprised Julia by suddenly going behind the counter and taking her hand.

Julia tried to pull it away and found that she couldn't. He was holding on to her hand rather tightly. "What are you doing?"

"Listening to your mother—like you should," Liam answered. Looking over his shoulder at Annie, he smiled. "See you later, Mrs. Tierney."

"Make it as 'later' as you like, Liam," Annie urged.

"Mother!" Julia cried. Okay, her mother *had* to know. But how? She hadn't said a word.

"She's stubborn," Annie told Liam as the rest of the customers in the store looked on in barely veiled amusement. "So you have your work cut out for you."

"I already know that, ma'am," Liam replied, ushering a protesting Julia out of the store.

The bell sounded, announcing their departure. Julia could have sworn she detected the faint sound of applause coming from the inside of the Superette and sending them on their way.

The color in her cheeks deepened.

Chapter Thirteen

Once they were outside and clear of the Superette, Julia slanted an uncomfortable glance toward Liam to try to guess his reaction to what had just transpired in the store.

"She knows," she said, referring to her mother.

She'd get no argument from him, Liam thought. "Your mother's a sharp lady. I suspect she probably does. Question is, how much does she know?"

Did the fact that her mother knew annoy him? Or did it just add notches to his figurative belt? Either way, she wanted Liam to know one thing. "I never said anything."

"I never said you did."

He didn't see her as the type who had to share every intimate detail with someone. He'd known more than his share of *that* type, the ones who relived their relationships by going into great detail with every girlfriend they knew.

"But some mothers have a way of just looking at you and intuiting things whether you want them to or not. I've got a hunch that might describe your mother. Is that a problem for you?" he asked. Unless he missed his guess, Julia seemed to be rather upset or flustered about the exchange that had just taken place with her mother inside the store.

Julia shook her head. She wouldn't exactly call being embarrassed by her mother a problem; she just didn't know *what* to label it. "No."

"Oh." He wasn't 100 percent sure if he believed her. "Because you look a little upset."

She supposed she did at that. "If I am, it's for you."

Why would she be upset for him? It didn't make sense. "Now you lost me."

That'll happen all too soon, Julia couldn't help thinking.

Out loud she explained her reasoning to him. "I just don't want my mother asking you a lot of questions, that's all."

Was that all? Liam grinned. "Don't worry about that. I can hold my own with your mother. Besides, she's a nice lady."

Well, at least he didn't hold grudges, Julia thought as she realized that she had gotten sidetracked by the exchange between her mother and Liam.

"You said you wanted a word with me," she reminded him. "About what?"

He looked at her for a long moment. The early afternoon sun wove its way through her hair, giving the red strands a golden sheen. He wondered if she realized that she was beautiful.

"I wanted to know if you wanted to see me tonight," he told her. Then, before Julia could answer him, he continued, "Because I want to see you."

Had she been slated to go out with some girlfriends, or attend a school reunion, she would have found a way to postpone it or beg off to go wherever he wanted her to go. Julia was well aware that it wasn't very independent of her, to be willing to rearrange her life because of a man, especially one with the sort of reputation that Liam had.

But frankly, she couldn't help herself. Being with him was like holding a bit of stardust in her hand. It was all magical and for as long as she could savor the experience, she intended to make the most of it. It would be over with soon enough and she didn't want to do anything that would hasten its demise or curtail its very short life expectancy.

She needed the memories to last her for the rest of her life because she instinctively knew that nothing, *nothing* was ever going to hold a candle to what she was experiencing with Liam.

"Is this the part where I'm supposed to be coy?" she asked when Liam paused, waiting for an answer.

He laughed. She was refreshingly devoid of any game playing. He liked that. "No, this is the part where you're supposed to say, 'Yes, Liam, I'd like to see you, too.'"

Julia grinned. "'Yes, Liam,'" she echoed, "'I'd like to see you, too.'"

His eyes were smiling as he regarded her. "Nice to know we're of like mind," he told her. And then a bemused expression came over his face as he cocked his head ever so slightly.

Was he waiting for something more? Or having second thoughts about what he'd just said? "What's wrong?" She wanted to know.

"Nothing's wrong," he told her. The grin was back and it grew wider. "I just never realized that you've got dimples. Two tiny ones," he went on. "Right there. And there." He lightly passed his forefinger along first one dimple, then the other, one at either corner of her mouth.

The moment his finger touched her skin, Julia could feel the longing beginning all over again, spreading a blanket of fire all along her body.

Abruptly he dropped his hand to his side.

When he saw her raise her eyebrow in a silent question, he explained, "I think I'd better stop touching you when we're out in public—because that might lead to kissing you and you wouldn't want people talking about you."

"I never cared about what people had to say," she told him honestly. There were people who were given to gossip and those who couldn't care less. Her friends wouldn't care and the others didn't matter.

"I do," he told her solemnly.

"Bad for your reputation?" she asked, curious.

He surprised her by saying, "No, bad for yours."

Julia blinked. "You're worried about my reputation?" she said incredulously.

He was accustomed to people talking about him because of his penchant to love 'em and leave 'em. Talking about Julia, though, was another thing entirely. He felt protective of her. Another new feeling for him. Being with Julia ushered in a series of "firsts," he couldn't help thinking.

"One of us should be."

Damn him, Julia thought.

Despite all of her silent lectures to herself, she could feel it happening. Could feel herself falling in love with Liam even though she knew there was no future for her in his life.

Falling for Liam was just about the worst possible mistake she could make.

And even though she knew that what he was saying to her was a line—he sounded so sincere, that just for a moment, she allowed herself to believe him.

He wanted to see her. She hugged that thought close to her heart.

"Why don't you come by my place tonight and I'll make you dinner?" she suggested.

Liam smiled and suddenly her immediate world seemed to light up. "I'd like that," he told her.

Not half as much as I will, Julia thought.

"I'd better be getting back," she told him. "Before my mother starts wondering what happened to me."

"If it came to that, I think she'd probably have a pretty good idea," Liam suggested. He turned his attention to what she'd said earlier. "What time tonight?"

"Eight?" It was more of a question than a statement. "It'll be after I close the store."

"Eight it is," he repeated with a nod. "Oh, and, Julia?" he called out just as she turned away.

She stopped and started to turn around to face him again. "Yes?"

Liam had crossed the short distance she'd managed to create between them and was right behind her as she turned, catching her off guard. The next moment he surprised her further by brushing his lips against hers.

Right where anyone could see them.

He grinned down into her face. "I figured it was okay," he teased, "since you don't care about people talking."

At this point, there *were* no other people in the world besides the two of them. For two cents she'd grab him by his shirtfront, pull him down to her level and kiss him long and hard.

She didn't do it. Not because of the people who were around, but because she knew that kissing him that way wouldn't satisfy her, it would just make her want even more. So she struggled to control herself as best she could.

"I don't," she murmured.

And then she was gone.

But as she hurried away, she could feel Liam's eyes on her.

Watching her.

Julia was grinning fit to kill by the time she walked back into the Superette.

* * *

The next afternoon found the Two Moon Saloon filled to capacity with people.

Unlike in some towns and larger cities, where meetings were conducted in auditoriums that echoed with apathy and little else, apathy did not have a seat here in the saloon in Horseback Hollow. Everyone prided themselves on taking a keen interest in civic affairs as well as in matters that affected the town's welfare. They'd come to realize that the concept of growth was more enticing than maintaining a status quo no matter how quaint that status quo might be in some people's eyes.

The meeting had been going for over an hour and when the mayor had thrown open the floor for a final discussion before the vote was taken, a number of people had come up to the makeshift podium in front of the bar to express their thoughts about the proposed restaurant.

Some spoke a little, others spoke more. And then the mayor turned toward Julia and asked if she had anything further to add.

She banked down her nervousness—this wasn't the time to indulge herself—and said that she did.

Coming up to the podium, she looked out at the sea of faces and told them what was in her heart.

"In this day and age," Julia said as she addressed the people at the meeting, "if a town doesn't grow, it shrinks and the outcome of that is obvious. Horseback Hollow means too much to all of us for us to watch it wither away on the vine.

"However, our choices have to be made carefully.

We can't just jump at the first offer that comes our way without examining all sides. Everything should always be examined and that includes weighing the pros and cons of inviting Wendy and Marcos Mendoza to bring their restaurant here to us.

"I know some of you are worried that we'd be sacrificing our way of life, become too 'citified' and so give up the warm, friendly atmosphere we all grew up with. That's exactly why we wouldn't bring in a chain discount store, or some big-name drugstore that cares more about profit than service. I can personally tell you that the Mendozas are good people and they're associated with good people. I'm referring to the Fortunes. The latter have no desire to use this town, pick it clean of its assets and then move on to do the same to another town." She paused for a moment to allow her words to sink in—and to take a breath.

"If we welcome them here, they will treat Horseback Hollow the way they treat Red Rock—like it was their home. And to insure that that is never lost sight of, they've asked me to be their assistant manager," she told the people she considered to be her friends and neighbors.

A murmur of approval went up.

As she spoke, Julia glanced more than once in Liam's direction. Each time she crossed her fingers behind the podium, hoping for a positive response.

To her relief, Liam appeared to be comfortable with what she was saying, unlike the first time when he'd walked out of the meeting when he saw that the preliminary vote was going her way.

When she was finished—having spoken longer than she'd intended—Julia left the floor open to any dissenters who wanted to air their last-minute thoughts. But there weren't any when the mayor called for any further comments or discussion before the vote.

"Well, if nobody else has anything further to say," he announced, "then I guess it's time to take the final vote. All in favor of the Mendozas' restaurant being built here in Horseback Hollow, raise your hands."

When a sea of hands went up, the mayor dutifully counted each and every one of them.

From the looks of it, it appeared that most of the people there welcomed the restaurant's construction. But bound by rules, the mayor called for a show of hands from those who opposed the restaurant being built in town.

"All opposed?" Several hands, totaling no more than nine, went up. He counted out each one.

"I guess it's settled then," the mayor told his constituents fairly confidently. "Looks like the ayes have it," he said to the people assembled in front of him. Then, raising his voice, he declared, "The measure to build a new restaurant here in Horseback Hollow is passed," and banged down the gavel to make it official.

"Meeting's adjourned," he announced needlessly since everyone was getting up anyway, talking to their neighbor, calling out across the aisles. It was obvious that despite the few dissenters, everyone appeared to have been won over by the idea of having a brand-new enterprise make a home in their town.

To a person, they looked forward to the pick up in

business that was sure to occur as a by-product of the restaurant's location.

Having taken a seat in the rear of the saloon so as not to call attention to himself, Liam had quietly taken in the proceedings as they'd unfolded. He knew that he'd surprised a few people by not speaking up when opposing viewpoints were requested.

Maybe he'd even surprised himself, as well.

The fire he'd felt initially in his belly concerning the matter eluded him now, having died out in the face of other things.

Talking to his father the other day had made him take a second look at his own feelings about being connected to the Fortunes. While he doubted that out-and-out jealousy had been behind his initial reaction to the discovery that his mother was one of them, he was willing to admit that he might have been more than a tad unreasonable, allowing his view of the situation to be tainted and made prejudicial by what he *thought* the Fortunes were like rather than finding out the truth of the matter for himself.

But he had to admit that the lion's share of what had actually changed his mind for him about the matter was Julia herself. If someone like Julia could be so in favor of an issue, then that issue deserved, at the very least, closer scrutiny.

With that in mind, he'd done a little research of his own into the matter by talking to Gabriella, Jude's fiancée. Gabriella, a Mendoza herself, had nothing but good things to tell him about the Fortunes, as well as her cousins. Julia was right.

The couple behind the new restaurant—not to mention the Fortunes themselves—*were* good people. And Wendy Fortune Mendoza was related to him and so she was family in the best possible sense of the word, he supposed.

Liam was *not* so naïve as to think that just because someone was family that automatically made them good people. He'd seen enough of the other side of that coin to know that was definitely *not* a given.

But these people liked to give back to any community they were part of and he liked that.

Ultimately he had a gut feeling that this restaurant that Julia was championing would be good for Horseback Hollow. Just as he had a gut feeling that Julia was the one woman he could see himself sharing forever with.

That had never been on his agenda. He'd just assumed that he would always remain free and untangled, able to go from woman to woman and dally for as long as it suited him, then just move on when the whim hit.

And now all he wanted was to be tangled up with her. Permanently.

Last night's lovemaking was still fresh in his mind. The mere thought of it sent his pulse up to a higher rate. But he didn't want to just look forward to their next evening together, the next time they made love together. He wanted to know that he could look forward to forever, that she would always be there whether he was thinking about the next evening, the next week, the next year or the next decade.

The more he reflected on it, the more he *knew* that she was the one for him.

He supposed, now that he thought about it, that this was what love, what *being* in love, felt like. Wanting one person to be part of your forever and wanting them to want you to be part of theirs.

Who would have ever thought he could feel this way? Liam marveled, swallowing a laugh that would only call unwanted attention his way. This was Julia's victory and she deserved to bask in it.

Flushed, thrilled, now that the meeting was adjourned and the vote was part of the town's history, Liam watched as Julia plowed her way through the milling bodies within the saloon to reach him.

She was positively glowing, he thought.

Liam slipped his arm around her the second she reached him. "Victory looks good on you," he told her, brushing his lips against her cheek. All he could think about was whiling away the night lost in her embrace and making love with her.

"You're not mad?" she asked, peering up into his face. She was surprised—not to mention relieved—that he was taking defeat so well.

"How can I be mad about something that makes you look so happy?"

But the din in the saloon had risen by several decibels as people were trying to out-shout each other. Unable to hear him because of the noise, Julia shook her head and pointed to her ear, indicating that she hadn't heard him.

Liam merely laughed, pulled her a little closer to

him. Bending over her ear, he said, "Let's get out of here."

That, she heard, as a wide grin blossomed over her lips. His suggestion was music to her ears. Julia was more than willing to follow him anywhere he wanted to go.

Chapter Fourteen

Julia felt as if she was literally walking on air and was seriously entertaining the idea of putting rocks in her pockets to keep from just floating away like a helium party balloon gliding on the wind.

It was the day after the vote and she was standing in front of what in a larger town would have been referred to as a vacant lot. At the very front of the lot was a sign driven into the ground by a wooden stake.

It was a large, no-frills sign that proclaimed the vacant lot to be only temporary because this site had been chosen as the "Future Home of The Hollows Brasserie."

I did it, Julia thought with no small enthusiasm or pride.

She had gotten everyone in town to come around and see how advantageous it was to have new business, new blood, come into Horseback Hollow. And because the restaurant was now destined to become a reality, she was going to finally—*finally*—realize her dream of running a restaurant and being, for all intents and purposes, in charge of its kitchen.

Granted, she wanted to run her *own* restaurant, but she knew that the path from here to there required a great deal of patience as well as baby steps. She was more than prepared to execute both, learning everything she could as she went. And this was really a very large step in the right direction.

That part of her future looked rosier than it ever had before.

As for the other part, well, Julia was fairly certain that the words to describe how happy she was hadn't been created yet.

She and Liam had gone to his ranch after the meeting last night and she'd cooked a meal for him—something she'd created on the spur of the moment out of things she found he had as leftovers in his refrigerator. She'd been inspired as she chopped and stirred and blended, but she really had no idea how her creation turned out because halfway through the preparations, she gave up trying to concentrate on what she was doing on the stove. Her mind kept insisting on wandering because of what Liam was doing to her with his hands and with his lips.

Between his caresses and his kisses, she'd gone from being a creative, independent young woman who had just experienced a major victory to a woman who had become all but completely liquefied.

Certainly unable to stand with any sort of demonstrable balance.

The only thought in her head at that point was that she wanted him. She gave up chopping, gave up stirring and blending and barely had the presence of mind to turn off the stove before she gave herself completely up to Liam and the magic that was him.

Last night it was as if they had both tapped into some secret source of energy because the lovemaking went on and on, encompassing the entire night.

Oh, there were breaks in between, but they were so small, they hardly counted.

What counted was that he wanted her as much as she did him. Even after having been with one another almost every night for two weeks, he hadn't grown tired of her, hadn't made love once or twice and then just rolled over to fall asleep. His energy seemed boundless, coaxing the same from her.

Consequently, as she stood admiring the sign that she assumed either Mayor Osgood or possibly even one of Marcos Mendoza's employees had put up, she felt both exhausted at the same time that she felt utterly exhilarated.

She had to be getting back to the Superette, Julia silently told herself. She wasn't the assistant manager of the still-to-be-constructed restaurant yet and until she was, her mother needed her to be working at the family business.

But Lord, Julia thought, sporting a huge smile, she did like looking at this pristine, sleek sign and its whispered promise of things to come in the very near future.

As she stood there, various people had passed by, taking note of it, marveling at how fast the sign had gone up and wondering out loud whether the restaurant would be built just as quickly.

Some sounded excited about the proposition, some seemed to be oblivious to its implications and still others were not overly ecstatic about the idea.

Such as the last duo she heard talking.

"'Future Home of The Hollows Brasserie,'" a low voice behind her read out loud to his companion. "What the hell is a Brass-y-yearie?" he mocked.

Julia was going to answer, but the man's friend did it for her.

"I think that's a restaurant where you don't have to order no food just to be able to order a drink."

"Huh," the first man snorted. "We already got that. It's called the saloon," the man said, referring to the Two Moon Saloon, where they had all voted yesterday. It was obvious by his tone of voice that he was not impressed and would rather the whole thing just go away.

That was his right, Julia thought, but she was very glad he and his friend were not in the majority.

"Guess the Two Moon ain't snooty enough for the Fortunes," the first man said. "And I bet that Liam was ticked off that his little plan didn't work."

"What plan?" the first man asked as they began to walk away.

"Well, he figured if he sweet-talked that gal who was pushing it—you know, the one who runs the Superette—and threw in a little loving to boot, she'd come around and see things his way. You *know* what that guy's like when he pours on the charm. Ain't a woman alive who can resist Liam Jones once he gets going."

"Well, looks like this Julia person did, though," his friend commented as their voices faded away.

Julia stood there, staring at the sign as the two men walked away. But this time, she really didn't even see it. Her vision was blurred with angry tears and she was unable to move—afraid to move because she felt physically sick and was afraid that one wrong step and she was going to throw up.

Literally.

Did everyone know about Liam's "plan"?

Was she the laughingstock of the town?

But she'd thought he loved her—

She'd thought—

Damn it, she *hadn't* thought and that was the problem, Julia upbraided herself. She'd gone leading with her heart, not her head in this.

More than that, she'd convinced herself that someone like Liam—the eternal "bad boy"—could have feelings, actual *feelings* for someone like her.

Just how stupid could she be?

Taking in a slow, deep breath and then releasing it, Julia did what she could to try to get hold of herself and her shattered ego. All she wanted to do was to crawl into a hole and die, but she couldn't indulge herself and just take off to cry this huge, searing, gaping pain away.

If she didn't turn up at the store soon, her mother would come looking for her and she couldn't have that sweet woman finding her like this.

Damn, but this hurt.

She'd remained in Horseback Hollow, giving up her dreams and her education, to provide support, someone to lean on, for her mother. In short, a solution to Mother's problem.

Solutions weren't supposed to generate their own set of problems.

At least, *she* wasn't going to create any problems, any waves. She was *not* going to let her mother see her cry or suspect that she'd just had her heart literally cut out of her chest.

All right, she'd survive this, she consoled herself, using the back of her hand to quickly wipe away the telltale tracks of her tears. Besides, she still had the restaurant to look forward to.

Somehow, that seemed like a very small consolation prize in comparison to what she'd *thought* she'd had in the palm of her hand just a few short minutes ago.

Served her right for believing that love actually conquered all. All it had conquered, to her huge regret, was her.

"I think you better get down there and exercise a little damage control—or maybe a lot," Toby told his brother without any preamble as he walked into Liam's stable looking for him.

Liam looked at him, surprised to see his brother here. They had no project set to do and as far as he knew, Toby was busy with work on his own place.

Obviously what he was talking about seemed important enough to Toby for him to come out here looking for him. He could have saved himself a trip.

"If you're talking about that restaurant coming here, I've decided not to fight it anymore." Liam grinned, thinking of last night and the way Julia had felt in his arms.

As though he had come home. Julia was his "home."

He finally, *finally* understood what it was that his brother Jude found so compelling about this thing called love, *real* love. The real thing—and this felt like it was—was absolutely, mind-blowingly wonderful. He was only sorry that it had taken him so long to find it— especially when it turned out to be right under his nose.

"No, I'm talking about your little plan coming to light," Toby stressed, disapproval imprinted on his handsome features.

Liam stopped mucking out the stall and stared at his younger brother. "What little plan? What are you talking about?"

Toby sighed. He didn't like to have to say this out loud. It seemed beneath Liam somehow—even though it sounded like the "old" Liam. "The plan to seduce Julia and get her to see things your way."

Liam frowned. He didn't bother saying he'd gotten caught in his own trap. That was self-evident to him and anyone in his life who mattered. Right now, there was something more important on the drawing board.

His eyes narrowed. "How do you know about that?" He wanted to know. While he'd initially intended to make Julia come around through unorthodox meth- ods, he had never said a word about it to anyone that he knew of. If someone was shooting off their mouth about it, it had to be from pure conjecture, not something he'd actually said.

It pained Toby to have to say this to his brother. He'd seen a change in Liam these past two weeks. A change for the better. He was less caustic, far more cheerful. He'd actually caught Liam whistling a time or two. He didn't want this new, improved Liam to just disappear.

"Buck Holt was shooting off his mouth about your plans to 'seduce' Julia to one of his friends and you know how fast word spreads around here."

He could feel his heart quickening with anxiety. It didn't matter that he hadn't said anything to Buck. This was bad.

"You think Julia knows?"

"Unless she fell into a coma early this morning, yeah, I think she knows. What the hell were you thinking, trying to pull off something like that?"

"I wasn't thinking," he protested. "And I didn't try to pull it off. I abandoned that harebrained scheme before I ever tried to do anything with it."

Toby looked at him skeptically. "Before or after you slept with her?"

This was getting to be positively unnerving. Did *everybody* know everybody else's business? "How do you know about *that?*" Liam demanded.

He hadn't told *anyone* he'd slept with Julia. Had she confided in someone? It didn't seem likely, but right now, everything was in such a state of confusion for him—not to mention red alert—that he didn't know what was up and what was down.

"Wasn't exactly hard to figure out," Toby told him.

"She had that 'touched by Liam Jones' glow that three-quarters of the girls in the graduating senior class had. Don't forget, I was right behind you in high school," he reminded Liam.

To his surprise, Liam tossed aside the rake he was using and hurried out of the stable to where he had left his truck parked early this morning, after taking Julia back to her home.

"Hey, where are you going?" Toby called out, raising his voice.

"To see about that damage control you mentioned," Liam shouted over his shoulder.

Gunning the engine, Liam threw the transmission into overdrive and all but flew the entire distance from his ranch to Horseback Hollow and the Superette.

He had to make this right, he thought. This just couldn't end like this, here, today.

It *couldn't*.

This had to be what they meant by that saying about sins coming home to roost. Liam didn't consider himself a sinner per se, but he had pretty much taken what he wanted out of life and enjoyed all the advantage of being handsome coupled with an ability to say exactly what women wanted to hear.

Oh, he never lied, never made promises he had no intentions of keeping just to get what he wanted, but that didn't exactly make him noble, either. Everything had come easy to him because of his looks and his charm. And the irony of it was that the one woman he really, really wanted he was now in danger of losing because of his past behavior—and someone's big mouth.

Maybe not, he tried to console himself. Maybe it wasn't as bad as it seemed. Maybe Julia wouldn't believe that he had tried to get her to come around by seducing her—

Why not? a voice in his head asked.

Be honest. Hadn't that really been the plan to begin with? To get her to come around to his side using any means that he could?

It wouldn't matter that the moment he began to be around her, everything had drastically changed. Wouldn't matter that he'd gotten caught up in her, in wanting to *be* with her.

In wanting to see her happy.

The damage was done and that would be all that she'd see, all that she would focus on. She was, after all, only human, not a saint.

He should have leveled with her from the very start, Liam lectured himself. But he hadn't wanted to risk it. Instead he had hoped that if he'd let things ride, they would eventually go his way because everything else always had.

And since he had eventually found himself on the same side of the debate about the restaurant as she was, he felt that there was no point in letting Julia know that he had had less than honorable intentions when he'd undertaken this whole campaign.

The truth was highly overrated, he couldn't help thinking.

Look what the truth was about to do to him—it was going to torpedo the first real love he'd ever felt right out of the water.

Part of him wanted to lay low and wait for this to blow over. But that was the coward's way out and beneath him, he silently insisted as he watched his speedometer edge up to eighty.

It wasn't worthy of him—or of her.

He arrived in town faster than he'd thought possible. Drawing his courage to him, Liam parked his truck across the street from the Superette and got out. His knees shook as he walked toward the Superette, trying to figure out just how he was going to say what he needed to say to save what they had between them.

His mind temporarily went blank for ten terrifying seconds.

This had to work. Even if he had to get on his knees, this had to work. He couldn't think about it going the other way.

The bell tinkled, announcing his entrance. Julia automatically glanced toward the door.

Damn it, Julia thought, her heart wasn't supposed to leap up like that anymore at the sight of Liam, not when she knew what was behind that smile, behind those compelling blue eyes that had come close to being her undoing.

She had to remember that Liam didn't care about her. He'd probably spent the morning laughing about the way she'd become almost like the proverbial putty in his hands. He had tried to play her and he had almost made her into a laughingstock.

The thought stung something awful.

She wanted Liam to feel what she was feeling, to know the pain of hurt, the sting of humiliation.

At a loss how to begin to broach this smoothly, he just stumbled in with an apology. "Look, Julia, I didn't mean to—"

Her eyes were frosty as she looked at him. "If you're trying to apologize, there's no need to."

He wasn't going to take the easy way out. He could see that he'd hurt her and she was angry. "Yes, there is. I—"

"There's no need to," she repeated, continuing as if Liam hadn't tried to interrupt. "Because, obviously, what you were attempting to do didn't succeed. Not that it was a bad plan," she allowed loftily, totally confusing him given the expression on his face, "but you didn't count on the fact that two can play that game."

His confusion only intensified. It felt as if someone had taken his brain to use as a tennis ball and had just lobbed it far into the air.

"What are you talking about? What game?" he asked.

Because people were beginning to stare, she tugged Liam over to the side, away from prying eyes. "To keep it simple, we can call it 'victory by seduction.' I think that rather sums it up nicely, actually." Her eyes bored straight into him. "You think that you're the only one who uses seduction as a tool to persuade an unwitting person of something?"

He stared at her, dumbfounded. What was she saying?

He didn't have long to wait for an answer. "While you were trying to play me, I decided to turn the tables on you and seduce *you* into seeing things my way." Her smile was cool and never even came close to reaching her eyes. "And, seeing as how the vote went my way and the sign for the new restaurant went up this morning, I'd say I turned out to be better at this little 'persuasion' game than you were."

She pretended to laugh even though the sound tore at her throat.

"In all fairness, I guess you didn't realize that I had it in me—but I did," she told him. "So you see," Julia concluded, "there's no reason to apologize. What you did just activated what I had to do. And I did it. You didn't oppose me and now the restaurant's going to be built."

Was she being truthful? Had she really played him, gotten him to come around by playing up to him, by making him think of nothing else, *want* nothing else, but her?

Liam felt as if someone had rammed a knife into his gut and then twisted it. Hard.

"Congratulations," he rasped.

"Thank you," she replied in the same dead tone he'd just used.

She turned away, walking back to the register, pretending that she was needed back at work.

Julia didn't need to look over her shoulder to know that he was walking out. She heard the bell signal his departure. It almost sounded mournful to her.

Victory had never felt as hollow as it did this minute.

That was okay, she told herself. She'd get over this by and by.

In about fifty years or so.

Until then, she thought, squaring her shoulders and marching to the register, she had customers to wait on.

Chapter Fifteen

Five days went by. Five long, agonizing days that seemed to drag by in slow motion, leaving long, jagged, painful scars in their wake.

Julia found she had trouble concentrating. It wasn't that she would drift off; it was more a case of her mind going blank with nothing for her to catch hold of. That, at least, was more merciful than other moments when she would berate herself for being such a fool. For being so incredibly naïve.

She'd been smarter, she told herself as despair would start to fill every nook and cranny in her being, when she had been in high school than she was now. Back in high school, she'd made a point of deflecting Liam's attention that time it had been directed at her.

Granted, when he had asked her out, it hadn't really

come across as a full-fledged attack on her defenses, but at the time she'd been more than relatively inexperienced. And yet she'd been smart enough to say "No" to him when all the other girls in school had cried a breathless "Yes!"

She might secretly have been a little miffed when he didn't try to get her to change her mind and had just shrugged in response to her rejection, but she'd been proud of herself then. Proud of the fact that she hadn't just followed the crowd like some brainless lemming and gloried in whatever small crumb of attention Liam would have been willing to give her at the time.

The bottom line was that she'd been discerning and she had made her mark on him by being the only one who'd turned him down, the one who *hadn't* worshipped at his feet.

And where did that get her? Years of unconsciously wondering what it might have been like to be with him? Being ripe for his romantic advances when they finally materialized in full force? That didn't exactly seem like much of a triumph to her.

And now what?

Now that she felt like a hollowed-out shell of her former self, what exactly was she to do with herself? Now that she knew what it felt like to be on the receiving end of his touch, his kiss, his exquisite lovemaking, where did she go from here?

How did she go on knowing that the very best was behind her and that she had nothing but emptiness in front of her?

Frustrated, Julia wiped back one offending tear, silently forbidding herself from shedding any more.

A lot of good *that* did, she thought unhappily. She was just grateful they had closed for the evening and that there were no customers to witness her meltdown.

No one, that is, except for her mother.

Julia turned her head away, hoping her mother hadn't noticed the telltale tears before she had a chance to wipe them away.

But she should have known better. Her mother was one of those legendary eyes-in-the-back-of-her-head mothers and was almost always one step ahead of her.

"I hate seeing you like this," Annie told her, her voice throbbing with sympathy. She had given Julia five days to deal with whatever was going on in her life, but she couldn't bear it any longer and broke her silence as they closed up the store. "Maybe if you tried to talk to him—"

"No!" Julia snapped, then flushed. "Sorry, I didn't mean to yell at you," she said in apology. "But really, Mom, I'm fine."

"No," her mother replied quietly but firmly, "you're not." She pointed out the difference. "When your marriage to Neal ended, you were fine. A little sad, yes, but you mustered on just as I knew you would. You *didn't* look the way you do now—"

Carrying the dairy products to the refrigerator in the storeroom, Julia sighed. "Mother, you're exaggerating."

"No, I'm observing," Annie corrected. "And if anything, I'm understating the situation.

"You and Liam looked good together. *Were* good

together," her mother stressed. "Some mothers sense things like that," she explained, "and I sensed it about the two of you."

Yeah, well, it was an act, all an act, Julia thought. And she, and her mother apparently, had fallen for it.

"He fooled us all, Mother. Liam is a very good actor."

But Annie shook her head. Her still vibrant red hair was cut short and swished around her face as if to underscore the sentiment she expressed.

"Not that good, Julia. My vision isn't colored by a desire for you to marry well or to nab a wealthy husband. My only, *only* requirement was—and is—for you to follow your heart, which was why I wasn't all that overjoyed when you told me you were marrying Neal."

The corners of Julia's mouth curved sadly. She'd expected her mother to be overjoyed by the news that she was going to marry the affable lawyer. Seeing sadness in her mother's eyes had only confused her.

"I remember," Julia said quietly.

"I *liked* Neal," Annie insisted. "He was a nice boy and he was obviously taken with you, but I knew that while you might have even talked yourself into loving him, you weren't *in* love with him and that, my darling daughter, makes a world of difference." She looked up into her daughter's eyes, trying to make her understand. "Julia, I'm not the wisest woman in the world, but I could see that you were in love with Liam—and you still are."

Denial quickly rose up in her throat and was hot on her lips, but Julia gave up the lie before she ever uttered a word. She knew there was no point to it. So instead, she shrugged, silently acknowledging her mother's statement.

"I'll get over it."

"I don't want you to get over it," Annie insisted, closing the refrigerator door with a little too much force. "I want you to act on it. Love is *not* all that common. It doesn't happen to everyone. And if it happens to you, you should make the most of it. Grab it with both hands and hang on for dear life."

Julia sighed again, struggling hard to keep from crying. "Mom, it's over. If Liam felt anything remotely close to what you're describing, he'd be over here, banging on my door, demanding to talk to me, demanding we work things out."

She pressed her lips together before going on.

"If you listen closely, you'll see that there's no banging, no demanding going on. There's *nothing*. It was all a charade, an act. And now it's over. He's gone. And I have a life to live."

Pausing for a moment, she kissed her mother's cheek. "Thanks for worrying, Mom, but please stop. That chapter of my life is closed. Now, I need to get some rest because I'm meeting with Wendy and her husband tomorrow. They said they wanted to talk to me about managing their restaurant." This was supposed to be one of the best moments of her life, better than she'd initially hoped. But she felt dead inside. Julia forced a smile to her lips. It wasn't as easy as it should have been, she couldn't help thinking as she took her mother's hand. "This is my dream, Mom. It's everything I've ever wanted. Be happy for me."

Annie squeezed her daughter's hand. She knew better, but right now, there was no point in beating this dead horse. "If that's what you want, Julia, then yes, of course, I'm happy for you."

But it was a lie.

Neither one of them was really happy.

"You going to hide in here forever?" Toby chided as he walked into Liam's stable the next morning.

Toby and his brothers and sisters had all gotten together to discuss their concern about the state of Liam's surliness as well as his withdrawal from sight for almost a week. When it came to the topic of which of them would approach Liam about the matter, they decided to draw straws.

As luck—or lack thereof—would have it, Toby had gotten the short one. That meant that it was up to him to approach Liam about it as well as to try to get him to abandon this hermitlike existence and get back into the game of life.

"I'm not hiding," Liam retorted. He didn't spare his brother a single glance. Instead he just went on brushing his horse.

"Nobody's seen you since the day after the vote was taken at the meeting—the day that somebody ran off at the mouth and started that stupid rumor about you trying to get Julia to see your way by seducing her," Toby pointed out.

"It's called working, Toby," Liam snapped at his brother. "I've been working. You should try it sometime."

"I work plenty, Liam," Toby reminded him patiently. "I run my ranch and I'm taking care of three kids and once in a while, I get to sleep for an hour or two. But we're not talking about me, Sunshine," Toby said sarcastically, "we're talking about you. Everyone in the family is worried about you. Nobody's seen you at the saloon and Stacey said you blew her off when she suggested meeting her at The Grill two days ago. She left a message on your machine. You never called her back."

Liam shrugged off the accusation. "Like I said, I've got work."

From what Toby could see, Liam might have work, but he hadn't done any of it. Except for one thing. "From the looks of it, you've groomed your horse to death, but the rest of the place looks like it's going to seed."

"If you're here to nag me, I'd just as soon you save your breath, turn around and ride back," Liam told him with finality. He might as well have flashed a no-trespassing sign at his brother for all the friendliness in his tone.

"Can't," Toby replied flatly.

Liam stopped grooming his stallion and fixed his brother with a look. "Why not?"

"'Cause," Toby said very simply, "I drew the short straw."

Liam narrowed his eyes, fixing his younger brother with a penetrating look. "And what's that supposed to mean?"

Toby went for the literal interpretation. "It means that we all drew straws to see who was going to come out to talk to you and I got the short one."

Liam could only stare at him in disbelief. "You drew straws," he repeated incredulously.

"Yeah," Toby replied. "Nobody likes talking to you when you're like this."

"Like what?" Liam challenged darkly.

"Angrier than a wet hen trying to peck at his dinner using a rubber beak."

Despite himself, Liam laughed a beat before his scowl returned. "Now there's an image," he mused. Then he sobered and looked at Toby. "Well, you talked to me. So you can go home now."

It didn't work that way, even though Liam's suggestion was tempting. "I'm not supposed to just talk. I'm supposed to get through to you," Toby explained. "Not that that's easy to do, given your thick skull."

"And just what is it that you're trying to 'get through' my thick skull?" he demanded. "What bits of wisdom are you and the others in possession of that you think you need to 'share' with me?" His voice fairly dripped of sarcasm.

This was a different Liam than the one Toby had grown up with and he didn't much care for this version. "That you're behaving like a jackass."

Liam set his jaw hard before answering. "Great. You've delivered the message. Now go," he ordered, trying not to lose his temper.

Toby and the rest of his family had no idea what he was going through and he wanted to handle recovering from it in his own way, not submitting to being burned by their "good intentions."

Toby refused to give up—or leave. Besides, he wasn't

finished yet. "And that Julia Tierney's the best thing that ever happened to your sorry ass and if you don't do anything to get her back, you're even dumber than I thought you were."

Though he didn't want to, Liam had to grudgingly admit that Toby had good intentions, even if he had his signals crossed.

"Put down your arrows, Cupid, there's nothing to 'get back.' Julia was playing me, trying to keep me distracted so that the vote for her precious restaurant would go through." He shrugged, pretending that what he was saying no longer hurt. "The second it did, she dropped me like a hot potato."

Toby frowned. "That's not the way I heard it."

"Well, that's the way it was," Liam told him flatly. "She *told* me that she played me. There was no point in hanging around after that."

"And you believed her?" Toby questioned incredulously.

Liam narrowed his eyes angrily. "Why shouldn't I believe her? There was no point in her lying to me about that."

Toby stared at him. Was he serious? "Are you familiar with the concept of saving face?"

Liam's scowl deepened. "What's your point?"

Toby tried to explain it as simply as he could. "Rumors are bouncing around all over the place that you were looking to get her to see things your way and you weren't above seducing her to make that happen. She hears that and then you show up at her store, so she does what any normal human being would do to save face. She makes up a story about turning the tables on you so that she doesn't come off being the butt of every joke for the next six months."

It was a good enough explanation—but there was just one thing wrong with it. "But the vote went her way," Liam insisted.

Toby dismissed the point. "That doesn't mean that you didn't have that plan up your sleeve. And with the vote going her way, she had something to build her lie on." He could still see skepticism in Liam's eyes. "Now, if you can't see that, then you're not nearly as bright as I always gave you credit for being."

Toby addressed the last words to the back of Liam's head as his brother went back to grooming his horse for the umpteenth time.

Liam didn't bother commenting, or even grunting.

Toby stood there for another couple of minutes, waiting for some sort of a response, but Liam went on ignoring him.

Finally, Toby sighed.

"Well, I've got a life to get back to. I forgot how damn stubborn you could be when you put your mind to it. It's like trying to dent a brick wall with a marshmallow," he told Liam with disgust. "Just remember, when you wind up alone at the end of the day, you've only got yourself to blame. I tried."

Liam went on maintaining his silence, grooming his horse as if he and the animal were the only two occupants inside the stable.

And eventually they were.

* * *

"Julia, please, sit down," Marcos Mendoza requested, rising to his feet the moment Julia walked into the hotel suite.

Julia had driven to Vicker's Corners to meet with Marcos and his wife since, as of yet, Horseback Hollow didn't have its own hotel. But maybe it would, Julia thought, now that the first step toward expansion had been taken.

"I know you know Wendy, but you haven't met our daughter, Mary Anne," he said, gesturing toward the pretty little two-year-old with the animated face and lively dark eyes.

"Very pleased to meet you," Mary Anne said, smiling up at her.

"You've got a little heartbreaker there," Julia told the couple. There was a trace of longing in her voice. She had always loved children and try as she might, she didn't see any in her future. Ever.

"Thank you, we like her," Wendy said with a great deal of affection as her arms closed around the little girl who had climbed onto her lap.

"We can't tell you how pleased we are to be building our restaurant in your town," Marcos began. "And I know we have a great deal to talk about. So I thought that the most efficient way would be if I just came out and asked you for your input and suggestions right up front." He smiled at her, not bothering to ask if she had any. His instincts about the young woman told him that she did. So he urged her on by saying, "Go ahead, I'm listening."

For some reason, the moment he said that, Julia thought back to the two men she'd overheard talking the morning she'd stood staring at the sign announcing the site of the restaurant's future home. The ones who had blown up her world.

One useful thing had come out of that hurtful exchange between the two men. "I was wondering if you've given any thought to changing the restaurant's name."

"The name?" he questioned. "You don't like the way the Hollows Brasserie sounds?"

"Oh, I think it sounds lovely," she told him quickly because she didn't want to offend him and because she actually did like the name. "But the trouble is Horseback Hollow isn't as cosmopolitan as Red Rock. Some people don't know what the word means at all, or think it's...well, a little lofty-sounding," she said, substituting *lofty* for the word *pretentious* at the last minute, again in an effort not to offend the man. "I was thinking of perhaps calling it The Hollows Cantina, you know, in keeping with the local atmosphere."

She watched Marcos's face, holding her breath. After all, he was the boss and as such, had the final say in the restaurant's name.

To her relief, he grinned after a moment, nodding. "Cantina," he repeated. "I like it. Just proves that we were right in choosing you to work here. You know these people better than we do, obviously, and that can only work to all our advantages," Marcos said, beaming.

Julia let go of the breath she'd been holding. At least

some things were going her way, she thought with a touch of sadness.

And if her heart still felt as if there was a bullet hole smack in the center of it, well, she'd just go on ignoring that sensation until she finally stopped noticing it altogether.

Someday.

But not today.

Chapter Sixteen

He hadn't been in town since he and Julia had gone their separate ways and he had discovered what it felt like to have his heart burned out of his chest while he was still breathing.

Because he'd been holed up on his ranch, Liam hadn't seen the sign he was standing in front of. The sign proclaiming this piece of land to be the "Future Home of The Hollows Cantina."

Liam assumed that the word *Cantina* had to have been an afterthought since it was written just above the now crossed-out *Brasserie*. Apparently either Julia or the Mendozas had decided a more down-to-earth name for the restaurant was needed.

He supposed that was progress of a sort.

There were other things written in on the sign, things

that had been inserted after the sign had been completed because they were written in rather than painted on. Like the words *Grand Opening.*

From what he could see, it was scheduled for a date two months in the future. On the left side of the sign were the words *Now Hiring,* which had to be a welcome sight for a number of people. Those were the ones who knew that ranching was *not* their true calling, but they still wanted to live in Horseback Hollow and earn a living. Jobs that didn't involve ranching were scarce around here.

This new cantina would make them less so.

"Congratulations, Julia," Liam murmured under his breath to the sign. "You did it. You got your restaurant."

"You know, talking to yourself out in public might be viewed by some folks as a person losing his grip on reality."

Liam didn't have to turn around to know that his brother Jude was standing behind him. Seemed as if he couldn't make a move without tripping over a relative, he thought in resignation.

"And sneaking up behind people is one surefire way to get the living daylights beaten out of them," Liam commented as he slowly turned around to face Jude.

"Guess it's lucky for me that you're so even-tempered," Jude joked.

"Yeah, lucky," Liam repeated in a less than cheerful tone.

The next minute Jude was asking him eagerly, "Did you hear the news?"

He'd obviously heard it as well as seen it, given

that he was standing in front of the sign boasting of it. "Yeah, the restaurant's going up," he answered Jude dourly.

For a second Jude stared at him, confused. The restaurant was *not* what he was referring to. "Well, yeah, that's news, too," Jude agreed even as he shrugged it off, "but it's old news."

"And you have 'new' news?" Liam asked with a touch of sarcasm.

In all honesty, Liam really wasn't sure *what* he was doing here in town, or what he had hoped to accomplish by coming.

He supposed that, deep down, he was hoping to run into Julia and get a dialogue going between them. He missed her, damn it, missed the sound of her laughter, the way her eyes sparkled. The way her hair smelled.

It almost seemed impossible, given that they had only been anything remotely resembling "a couple" for little more than two weeks. And yet, when he was with her, he felt as if he had come home, that he was finally whole.

And without her, he wasn't.

It was as simple as that and he could either make his peace with being without her—or do something about getting her back.

The latter wasn't going to be easy and he knew it. For that reason, he secretly welcomed this unexpected distraction that Jude offered.

"Yeah, I do have 'new' news," Jude told him, pleased that he knew something that Liam didn't. "And it involves Toby."

"What about him?" Liam was curious. And if it involved his other brother, why hadn't Toby come over or called and told him about whatever it was himself? Liam could only think of one reason he hadn't seen Toby. "Is he okay?"

Jude grinned and succeeded in annoying him even more than he already had. "Oh, he's more than okay. He's pretty damn happy and more than a damn sight relieved."

Liam struggled to hold on to his patience. "Are you going to tell me what's going on in bits and pieces or are you going to just come out and say it like any normal adult?"

Jude looked just a little put off by his attitude. "Anyone ever tell you that you're no fun?"

"Yeah, lots of people," Liam assured him. "Now talk," he ordered, trying not to allow his concern to show through. "What's going on with Toby?"

Jude did what he could to maintain an air of mystery about what he was revealing, doing so a layer at a time. "Well, somebody slipped an envelope under his door yesterday. It was full of money. A whole bunch of money."

Liam stared at his brother, his expression becoming a deep frown. "From who?"

"That's just the thing," Jude told him, the excitement in his voice growing again. "There was a note but it wasn't signed. It just said the cash was to help take care of the Hemings kids."

"Had to be someone in town," Liam assumed.

But Jude shook his head. "Toby really doesn't think so."

"Why?" There was only one reason for that, he realized. "Just how much money are we talking about?" When Jude told him, it was all Liam could do to keep his jaw from dropping. "You're right," he agreed. "Nobody around here has that kind of money to give away, no matter how good their intentions."

"Nobody but the Fortunes," Jude reminded him.

Liam banked down his automatic desire to dismiss the family because he didn't think of them as altruistic. But of late he'd been learning more and more about the Fortunes and realizing that his preconceived notions regarding them were not just unfair, they were downright wrong.

"How does Toby feel about being on the receiving end of charity?" Liam asked. Toby had every bit as much pride as he did. He'd always liked earning his own way. "Is he resentful?"

"Resentful?" Jude repeated with a laugh. "Hell, no, he's downright grateful. It's for the kids, after all, not him. And Toby doesn't see it as being charity so much as he sees it as being charitable." Jude looked at him for a long moment.

Long enough for Liam to know that something was on Jude's mind that the latter was chewing on. "You have something more to say?" he asked Jude.

"Yeah," he said, picking out his words slowly, the way he might pick his path through a minefield. "Don't you think it's about time you got over your grudge—whatever started it—and accept Mom's family? You know that Mom has. And even Dad finally has, in a way. You're the family holdout."

Shoving his hands into his back pockets, Liam sighed. Ordinarily he wouldn't have cared about being the lone holdout. But he couldn't do it if he'd been wrong to begin with. "Yeah, I guess they really are good people, after all."

"So," Jude began, humor dancing in his eyes, "you don't want to tar and feather them and run them out of town anymore?"

Liam shrugged, doing his best to keep a straight face. "I guess we can hold off on that for a while, seeing as how they *are* family and all."

"There's that generous soul of yours, coming through again." Jude pretended to marvel as he slapped him on the back. "Well, I'll let Mom know. Your change of heart will make her very happy."

"You do that," Liam murmured. "There been any takers?" he asked his brother, switching gears out of the blue.

"What?" Jude stared at him in confusion. "What kind of takers?"

Liam nodded toward the sign. "You know if anyone's applied for a job yet?"

"Why, you looking to branch out?" Jude teased.

The scowl that came over Liam's face had his brother backing off. "Just wondering, that's all," Liam said flatly.

"Why don't you go and ask Julia about it?" Jude suggested innocently. "She'd be the one to know." His eyes narrowed as he looked at his brother intently. The truth came to him riding on a lightning bolt. "You haven't gone to see her yet, have you?"

"I've been busy," Liam answered, a vague, dismissive shrug punctuating his reply.

It was Jude's turn to shake his head in absolute wonder.

"You're my older brother, Liam, and I've always looked up to you. I know you don't exactly welcome advice, but you're selling yourself a bill of goods if you think you can use that excuse indefinitely."

"You're right." Liam turned to look at his younger brother. "I don't welcome advice."

And with that, he got into his truck and drove back to his ranch instead of toward the Superette the way he had initially intended when he had driven into town.

It wasn't that he had lost his nerve—exactly, he told himself—it was just that he realized he still hadn't found the right words to use in framing his apology. He didn't want to come across as either a sap or some gutless, spineless cowboy.

And even though he missed her like crazy, he wasn't about to go crawling to her, either. For one thing, she wouldn't respect him if he did. For another, he wouldn't respect himself, either, and once respect was gone, there was nothing left.

So he went home, to stare at his phone and mull over his situation.

When he did finally pick up the receiver, it wasn't Julia that he called but her future boss. Marcos Mendoza.

The latter was surprised to hear from Liam and even

more surprised to hear the reason for Liam's unexpected phone call.

"You want to reserve *two* tables for the restaurant's grand opening?" Marcos questioned as if he was fairly sure he hadn't heard correctly.

But he had.

"That's what I said. Two," Liam confirmed.

"You do know that we're not opening for another two months, right?" He obviously thought the reservations were a bit premature, since the building hadn't even gone up yet. But Liam always liked being two steps ahead of everything.

"Yeah, I know," Liam answered.

Marcos quoted a cover charge and Liam remained unfazed, saying that was fine with him.

"Okay, consider them reserved," Marcos assured him.

Liam gave him all the particulars Marcos required— phone number, name, etc.—and then hung up.

And crossed his fingers.

"Two tables?" Julia questioned when Marcos called her about the reservation a few minutes later. "You sure it was Liam and not one of his brothers?"

"I'm sure. I verified it twice," he added. "You're off to a really good start, Julia," Marcos told her. He was obviously very pleased. "I just wanted to let you know," he concluded.

Julia thanked him as she hung up, more than a little stunned.

Had she misjudged Liam, after all? She needed to untangle this before it made her crazy.

"Mom," she announced, taking her coverall apron off and leaving it bunched up beneath the counter. "I've got to take off for a couple of hours. Think you can cover for me?"

"If I can't, I'm gonna have to learn, sweetie," Annie told her, patting her daughter's face. "Go, do what you have to do," she told her, all but shooing her out of the store.

Julia was out of the Superette and in her SUV within five minutes of hanging up with Marcos. Her destination was Liam's ranch, to corner the lion in his den to find out what sort of games he was playing now. Or had he changed his mind, after all?

She knew what she wanted more than anything was for Liam to come around, to have him on her side and wishing her well in this brand-new, exciting venture she was undertaking. Because, despite the fact that this was what she really wanted to do, she couldn't pretend that she wasn't exceedingly nervous about undertaking this project. Assistant manager of the first real restaurant in Horseback Hollow was a huge amount of responsibility, no matter how clear-eyed she was about the benefits of the venture.

Her hands were damp as she clutched the steering wheel and drove a little faster than was her custom to Liam's ranch. She was going to have it out with him once and for all. One way or another, this was all going to get resolved.

Today.

Her heart was pounding madly by the time she pulled up in his driveway. The thought had also occurred to her less than five minutes ago that he might not even be at the house. After all, he could be breaking in a horse, repairing a length of fence—perhaps even out somewhere, finding a new companion for his bed.

The last thought succeeded in making her stomach flip over and churn wildly, which in turn made her nauseous.

This was *not* the way she wanted to feel when she finally saw Liam for the first time in more than a week.

Searching for courage, Julia raised her hand to knock on the door only to drop it before her knuckles touched the wood. Not once, but twice.

The third time, she succeeded in making contact with the door. There was no answer. Taking a deep breath, she knocked again, harder this time.

There was still no answer.

Frustrated, she tried again, all but pounding on the door.

"Maybe I'm not home."

Julia jumped, stifling a scream with her hands over her mouth as she swung around. That deep voice seemed to echo all around her.

"Liam!" she cried breathlessly, her heart leaping up into her throat. She dug her fingernails into her palms, trying to force herself to calm down.

Liam cocked his head and looked at her. "I take it that you weren't expecting me."

Chapter Seventeen

It took Julia another thirty seconds before she could finally think straight. Even so, about 90 percent of her brain was still shrouded in a fog, offering only shadows for her to work with.

She found herself torn between wanting to throw her arms around Liam—and wanting to pound on him for putting her through this hell she found herself in.

Get a grip, Jules. Remember why you're here.

"Yes, of course I expected to see you, just not standing behind me," she told him coolly. "But then, you were never exactly predictable, were you?" She couldn't help adding the small dig. Given what she'd been through, Julia thought, she could be forgiven for being a little testy.

"Guess not," Liam replied. Circling around her, he

opened the front door and then took a step back. "Why don't we go inside and you can tell me why you're here. Unless," he added as an afterthought, "you'd feel safer standing outside."

Liam looked at her, waiting for her to make her choice.

Julia raised her chin, braced for a fight. Was he hinting that she was afraid of him for some reason? That certainly wasn't the case. They were still the same people they'd always been—basically.

So, instead of taking the bait—if that was what he intended it to be, she thought—she merely breezed by Liam and walked inside his house.

A smile played on his lips as he followed her in. Maybe things were not quite as dire as he'd thought.

Liam mentally crossed his fingers.

Maybe, just maybe, there was a glimmer of light coming into the coffin before it was nailed shut. Enough light to detect life if there was any to be had. Because as far as he was concerned, there was a *great deal* of life left in the romance that she had pronounced dead.

He just needed to convince her of that.

"Can I offer you something to eat or to drink?" he asked, letting his voice trail off so that Julia felt free to make her own suggestion if she was so inclined.

She did.

"You can offer me an explanation," Julia told him.

Liam closed the door behind him and then turned to face her. "About?"

Liam struggled to keep his voice as cool and distant as hers, but it was taking everything he had not to just pull her into his arms and kiss her the way he'd been aching to do ever since he'd walked out on her at the Superette.

Pride had made him go. But pride was a pretty damn poor substitute for a living, breathing woman who had his heart shoved into her back pocket and probably didn't even know it. Pride couldn't keep him warm at night, or make him happy in any manner.

He'd come to realize in these past few days that pride was an empty, hollow thing that was liable to break at any moment and when it did, it would reveal a gaping hole inside his chest and nothing more.

"Marcos called and told me that you reserved two tables for the Cantina's grand opening. Did you?" she asked.

His eyes met hers. There had to be more, he told himself. But for now, he'd answer Julia's question. "I did."

"That doesn't make any sense. You were completely against the restaurant being built here in Horseback Hollow. Are you planning on burning the place down on opening night?" she asked him point-blank.

Try as she might, she couldn't think of a single reason why Liam would have reserved one table, much less two, in a restaurant he had been so determined to sabotage in the first place.

What was he up to?

"No, Julia," Liam told her calmly. "I'm planning on eating."

Yeah, right. Julia regarded him suspiciously. "And you need two tables for that?"

Her gaze was meant to nail him to the wall. He never flinched. "I'm not planning on eating alone."

"Oh. I see," she said slowly, her mind casting around for a viable scenario. She saw the first thing that occurred to her. "Is this going to be some kind of a reunion of your last dozen or so girlfriends?" she asked coolly.

"No, it's not," he answered, never missing a beat. "I was thinking of having my family accompany me. You know, Jude and Gabi, Toby and those kids, my sisters and even my parents. I thought it might make a nice event for my family," Liam concluded, leaving her completely dumbfounded.

Julia shook her head. "I don't understand. You were so dead set against having this...*invasion,* I believe was the word you used—having this invasion coming into the town just a few weeks ago. Now you want to bring your family on opening night?" she questioned.

Liam took a deep breath, swallowed the last of his pride and told her, "I was wrong."

Julia blinked. Had she not been looking at his mouth as he'd said it, she would have sworn she was hearing things. But he had actually said that.

Still, she had to make sure she wasn't suddenly hallucinating. "You're admitting that."

His eyes never left hers. This was for all the marbles, he thought. The old Liam would have never gone this far. But he'd already lost everything. This was his only chance to gain it back and he knew it.

"Yeah."

Julia blew out a breath. "Okay, what's the catch?" She wanted to know.

There had to be a catch. Much as she wanted to believe Liam, much as she wanted to trust him, a part of her held back, afraid of being proved wrong yet again. She'd barely survived—if you could call it that—once. Twice would kill her.

"There isn't one. I'm telling you the truth," he swore. He *had* to make her believe him. "I've made more than my share of mistakes, Julia, and I don't want to make any more. And while I'm at it, here's another 'truth' for you—"

Julia braced herself, expecting the worst.

"You were right. I did start out romancing you to get you to change your mind about backing the restaurant." His eyes on hers, he prayed what he was about to say wasn't a mistake. But if he was to win her back, there had to be nothing but honesty between them. "I thought if I could get you into my bed, I could make you forget all about your project. Instead, *I* was the one who forgot all about it. The first time we made love, I realized that the only thing that really mattered to me was you—and," he admitted, "that pretty much scared the hell out of me."

She knew it took a lot for him to admit that. What she couldn't understand was why something as special as what they'd had would scare him. "Why?"

"Because I couldn't seem to control the feelings I had for you. Instead they were controlling me. So when you broke things off, telling me you had done the same thing that I had set out to do, part of me thought, okay, maybe it was better this way. I thought I could get over you."

"Like a cold," she concluded with finality. She tried

to appear indifferent to what he was saying, but the thought hurt.

He laughed shortly. He could see why she'd say that. Liam shook his head. "People get over colds," he replied. And he had certainly *not* gotten over her. "You're more like a fever of the blood."

"People get over fevers, too," she pointed out in a low voice, doing her best to contain her feelings.

Was it too late? she wondered, the thought all but squeezing the air out of her lungs. Was Liam telling her that he was "over" her?

"I haven't," he told her. "And here's another truth for you. I don't think I'm going to. Ever."

She took in a long, shaky breath. She knew how hard that had been for him. The least she could do was come clean herself.

"All right," she began, "since we're telling the truth, I might as well tell you that I lied, too."

"You?" he asked. He braced himself for anything. "About what?"

She would rather not look him in the eye when she said this. But to look anywhere else would have been cowardly. "About seducing you."

"But you did seduce me," he reminded her. And with no effort at all, she'd held him in the palm of her small hand.

"If I did, it wasn't to get you to forget about convincing people to vote against the proposal." She could feel her cheeks growing warm as they turned a shade of pink, but she pushed on. "My only ulterior motive was to get you to want me for a while longer."

Relief swept through him. He smiled at her then, his eyes caressing her, making love to her even though his hands remained at his sides. For now.

"You succeeded beyond your wildest dreams," he told her. "Because I do."

"You want me?" she asked uncertainly, afraid to hope. "After everything that happened?"

"More than I ever did," he admitted freely. "I want you now. I'll want you tomorrow and all the tomorrows for the rest of my life."

She looked at him, afraid that she was hearing what she wanted to hear and not what Liam was really saying. So, at the risk of looking like an idiot to him, she asked, "What are you saying, Liam?"

He'd never tripped over his tongue before. Words had come so easily to him because they'd required no thought and had no heart behind them. But everything was different now. His heart—and the rest of his life— were on the line.

"I guess, what I'm saying—awkwardly—is that I want you to marry me."

Julia's mouth suddenly went dry as she stared at him. It was as close to dumbfounded as she'd ever been. "You're proposing." It was half a statement, half a mystified question.

"I did mention that I was saying it awkwardly," he reminded her.

Her eyes smiled and then the corners of her mouth began to curve ever so slightly. "You want me to be your wife?"

"I could act it out with hand puppets if you'd like," he offered.

"What I would like," she told him, still careful to keep any emotion out of her voice, "is to have you make me understand why you're asking me to marry you."

He could see why she would be skeptical. He wasn't doing this very well. But then, he'd never done this before and in all honesty, had never thought he would. "Because I've seen what living without you after having you in my life is like and I hate it. I don't *want* to live without you anymore and I'll do whatever I have to, to get you to say yes."

He took a breath, then, carefully taking her hands in his, he looked into her eyes and said, "I love you, Julia. I've never said that to another woman—other than my mother and I think I was five at the time. Point is, I'll never say that again to any other woman. I don't want anyone else. I want you."

Julia was silent for a long moment, and when she finally spoke, she uttered a single word.

"Wow."

It wasn't the word he was hoping for.

Liam looked at her uncertainly. "Is that a yes? Because if it's not, I intend not to give up until it is. Just tell me what I have to do to get you to say yes and I'll do it," he promised. "Because—"

She put her fingers on his lips to still them. "You can shut up and kiss me," she told him. "And make love with me." Because as far as she was concerned, way too much time had passed since he had.

The grin that took possession of his mouth was almost blinding. He took her into his arms, pulling her closer. "I can do that."

And he did.

* * * * *

Start your free trial now

We Love Romance
with MILLS & BOON

Available at
weloveromance.com

LET'S TALK
Romance

For exclusive extracts, competitions
and special offers, find us online:

- **f** facebook.com/millsandboon
- 🐦 @MillsandBoon
- 📷 @MillsandBoonUK

Get in touch on 01413 063232

For all the latest titles coming soon, visit
millsandboon.co.uk/nextmonth

MILLS & BOON
MEDICAL
Pulse-Racing Passion

Set your pulse racing with dedicated,
delectable doctors in the high-pressure
world of medicine, where emotions run
high and passion, comfort and love are the
best medicine.

JOIN US ON SOCIAL MEDIA!

Stay up to date with our latest releases, author news and gossip, special offers and discounts, and all the behind-the-scenes action from Mills & Boon...

 millsandboon

 millsandboonuk

 millsandboon

It might just be true love...